Y0-CRR-189

The Search
for
Sara

Also by Martin Russell

Backlash

The Search for Sara

Martin Russell

Walker and Company
New York

First published in the United States of America
in 1984 by the Walker Publishing Company, Inc.
This addition printed in 1985.
Library of Congress Cataloging in Publication Data

Russell, Martin James, 1934–
    The search for Sara.

    I. Title.
PR6068.U86S4 1984   823′.914   83-40436
ISBN 0-8027-5584-4

Printed in the United States of America

10 9 8 7 6 5 4 3 2

CHAPTER ONE

The day was Sunday: the month was June: the weather was pure gold. That much I am clear about. All three factors, I remember thinking vaguely at the time, undoubtedly contributed to Sara's decision to go out. She had called to me from the hall.

'Just going for a stroll. Shan't be long.'

'Okay.' My reply may have lacked spontaneity. Most of my attention was absorbed by the Press accounts of the previous day's Davis Cup tie in Chile. I did surface in time to add, 'Anything to be seen to?'

'No. The oven . . .'

The rest had eluded me. Moments later the street door had clumped shut, and with a sense of enhanced restfulness I had returned to the shock defeat of the Swedish team by the unfancied South Americans on a court surface which was the subject of bitter complaint by the former.

It wasn't that I felt guilty about reading the newspapers on a Sunday morning. Sara had never resented the habit. Or, if she had, she had concealed the emotion with remarkable success for twenty years. It was simply that my own pleasure in relaxation received a fillip if I knew that she was relaxing as well. During the week I worked hard, and I could think of no good reason for not taking it easy when the chance came along; but a totally silent house, a rare luxury at that time, undeniably oiled the mechanism of the process. From the sports pages, I turned back to read of a self-employed lorry-driver who was faced with paying £23,000 damages out of his own pocket because, unwittingly, he had not been insured at the time of a collision. In an effort to comprehend the legal point at issue, I read the story twice before letting the newspaper slide to the floor and closing my eyes.

When next I glanced at my watch, the hands stood at twelve-forty. The sun had moved round to scorch the back of my neck. In a half-dreamy state I sat listening. Surrounding me was that peculiarly dense kind of silence which cannot be confused with mere absence of activity. Feeling dimly uneasy, I hoisted myself clear of the armchair and went out to the hall. A pale beige spring coat hung neatly folded across the arm of the telephone stand, so I relaxed and went through to the kitchen. Normally on a Sunday we lunched at about one.

The stench of over-roast lamb hit me as I entered. I examined the oven regulator: it stood at 250. I knew little about cookers, but I did know how a joint should smell. When I opened the oven door I was met by billows of fumes from a charred lump which looked as if it had strayed in from a barbecue staffed by pyromaniacs. It came out hissing. After sliding it on to a worktop to spit, I flung open the outer door to disperse the smoke, taking the opportunity to look for any sign of Sara among her cherished rosebushes against the west wall of the garden. She was nowhere in view.

Returning to the hall, I raised my voice. 'Sara? Did you know the joint was ruined?'

The encompassing silence was disturbed by the thump of the kitchen's outer door. Relieved, I made my way back. 'I was starting to— Oh Debbie, it's you. Any sign of Mum?'

'Isn't she here?' Our elder daughter's beam of greeting faded as she sniffed the air, spotted the blackened mound cooling in its pan. 'Disaster,' she exclaimed, advancing to inspect it. 'You'll be for it, Dad. What time were you supposed to switch it off?'

'I was given no instructions,' I said defensively. 'Your mother . . .' Thinking back, I shook my head. 'She just

said she was going for a walk and there was nothing to be
seen to.'

'What time was that?'

'Soon after ten-thirty.'

Debbie glanced at the wall-clock. 'Two *hours* ago?'

To combat her faint alarm and my own, I made a show
of revising my estimate. 'Later than that, probably.
Closer to eleven. Still, nothing alters the fact that she left
the oven turned too high.' I nodded at the ruin. 'What do
we do with that?'

'Ash is good for flowerbeds.' Donning protective gloves,
Debbie lifted the pan decisively and carried it outside.
'Not like Mum,' she remarked, returning after a few
moments and restoring the gloves to their hook. 'I've
never known her to burn anything before. Perhaps she's
called in at the Petersons' and forgotten the time.'

'The who?'

'Her buddies in Welling Avenue.'

'Never heard of them.'

'Oh Dad. She often talks about Dawn and Brian.
They're the big noises of the branch.'

'Branch?'

Debbie liberated a sigh. 'The Horticultural League.
You are aware she's the hon. membership secretary?'

'Ah. That.' I strove to look wise while feeling guilty. If
Sara had mentioned such an activity in my hearing, it
could only have been when I was deep in preoccupations
of my own, in no state to receive signals. Avoiding
Debbie's eyes, I added, 'Are they on the phone, these
Petersons?'

'Sure to be. But she'll only get in a flap if we call. Let's
give her a few more minutes.'

'How about lunch?'

Debbie gave me the tolerant faint smile of eighteen
male-conditioned years. 'No need to panic, Dad. We'll
eat.'

Her words and manner made me feel ninety instead of forty. I said restrainedly, 'There's no panic as far as I'm concerned. I can last another hour without dropping in a starved heap. Where's Carol?'

Tugging open cupboard doors, Debbie scanned the contents. 'Helping the curate. They're sorting out stuff for the church fête. She'll probably be late as well. You know she's potty about him?'

'The curate?'

Another sigh. 'Try mentioning Lionel to her some time. She goes all rigid.' Removing a can from a shelf, she held it up. 'Corned beef? I can do fritters.'

'Good girl.' Covertly I glanced at the clock. 'I think I'd better phone the Petersons.'

The ringing tone persisted for a while before the receiver was picked up. 'Yes?' snapped a male voice.

Disconcerted, I groped for a phrase. 'Is Mrs Brent there, by any chance?'

'Sara Brent?' The voice moderated itself. 'No, she's not. Who's calling?'

'It's her husband. I wondered —'

'She's not here, Mr Brent. We did speak to her last Friday.'

'She called round then, did she?'

'No, no. We were in touch on the phone. Did she say she was calling in this morning?'

'Not to my knowledge. It just seemed a possibility.' Detecting faint champing sounds, I added hurriedly, 'You're in the middle of lunch, I expect. I won't keep you. She probably —'

'If we do see her, we'll tell her you rang.'

'That's very kind of you.' I hung up. 'So much for that theory,' I observed, returning to the kitchen where Debbie was grappling with the can-opener. 'She hasn't been to the Petersons'.'

'Well, I dare say she'll be back any second.' Debbie's reply was light. 'An hour or two's walk wouldn't seem like much in this weather.'

Two hours and a half. I said the words silently to myself. Leaving her shaking corned beef on to a plate, I went to the street door and gazed out from the porch. As suburban residential thoroughfares go, ours is a not untypical specimen, boasting its due complement of mellow brick walls, unmade footways and overhanging foliage: on this particular morning it was unmistakably the motor advertiser's image of the British way of life, upper middle range division, with its Datsuns, Colts and Granadas berthed in the driveways, skins gleaming from detergent. One garden along, our neighbouring sales executive, Walter Freebody, was producing the ultimate sheen on his scarlet BMW and simultaneously acquiring one of his own by way of a shirtless upper torso. Glancing across, the tip of his long nose glinting in the sun's glare, he flapped his duster like a fan.

'Hot enough for you?'

'Glorious,' I called mechanically. His observations had the slick, lathe-moulded, mind-freezing efficiency of his chosen profession. His wife Amelia had once informed me that everyone liked Walter, which had tended still further to cloud my view of him ever since. In the interests of neighbourhood amity I added, 'That's a beautiful shine.'

'Comes up a treat, doesn't she?' He dealt the blazing bodywork a complacent slap.

'Sara doesn't happen to be with Amelia, I suppose?'

'With her?'

'In the house. Talking to her.'

'Amelia's in town, old boy. Some art show at the Barbican. Mislaid Sara, have you?'

'She's a bit late back from her walk.'

'Can't say I've seen her.' He massaged a corner of the

windscreen, perusing it from all angles. 'How long has she been out?'

'A couple of hours,' I hedged.

'Covering some ground, isn't she? Carried away by the conditions.' Hauling a clean rag from his car valet pack, he mounted an assault upon a side window, his long, thinning hair bouncing about his ears. 'If I see her,' he added, scowling into the glass, 'I'll tell her she's in big trouble with the family, tee-hee.'

'By then it won't matter.' With a parting flip of a hand I withdrew indoors, conscious of a weight at the base of my stomach. For a moment or two I stood looking at the phone, wondering who to contact. While I was debating, Debbie emerged from the kitchen wearing a green floral apron and a question mark.

'It's almost one-thirty.'

'What's happened,' I explained, 'is that she's tried out a new route and lost herself. We'll hear all about it when she gets back.'

'She could have rung,' said Debbie.

We both stood watching the phone.

'How are the fritters coming along?'

'Ready for frying.' She spoke half-heartedly. 'Dad, how about calling the Vicar? He could tell us whether—'

'It's all right,' I interrupted, the abdominal weight spreading wings and soaring off. 'I heard the side gate.'

'Thank heaven. I'm starving.' Debbie marched back to the kitchen. Smiling at myself and my cretinous panic, I returned to the living-room chair and the newspapers: Sara would scoff at any hint of consternation. I was turning to the political feature pages when I heard Debbie's voice again. Its pitch was a few tones higher. 'You've not *seen* her?'

My heart gave a lurch. Jettisoning the newsprint, I went outside. Carol, clad in dust-streaked cream cotton trousers, stood pink-faced in the hall, looking perplexed.

She turned appealingly to me.

'Did Mum say she was coming to look for me? I did warn her I might be late.'

'No, darling. She didn't say anything.' Trying to placate her and at the same time calm Debbie, who was visibly accumulating tension, I heard the shake in my own voice and had to cough to disguise it. 'She went for a walk and seems to be taking her time, that's all. Debbie has the lunch under control.' The breath I took was an audible one. 'How did the sorting go?'

Carol turned back to her sister. 'Have you tried the Petersons?'

'She's not been there. We were just about to ring the Vicar.'

'He's been with us,' said Carol. 'All morning.'

'Who else is there?'

'The Smythes? The Roper-Fenwicks?'

'Mum hardly knows them.'

'Does she have an address book? We could—'

'Now, girls, wait a bit.' My words were intended to strike a note of semi-humorous reproof; instead, they emerged as the bleat of a desolate ewe scouring a hillside for a lamb. 'No sense in swamping the switchboard. Even if we knew who to call, by the time we . . .'

I lost the thread of my argument. The eyes of both girls—the green, steady ones of Debbie and the unpredictable violet pair of her younger sister—were fixed upon me in ways that were as disparate as they were disconcerting. Debbie's harboured an odd, faintly accusative quality that I hadn't seen in them before: Carol's seemed to combine trust with dubiety in unfathomable proportions. Manifestly she was still adjusting to the notion that at one-forty on a Sunday her mother was nowhere in evidence at her domestic post. In her short-sleeved turquoise blouse, with a faint dirt-smear down one jawline, she looked less than her sixteen years. I had an impulse, which I resisted, to enfold her in a comforting arm.

The right attitude for the moment was hard to fix upon. Something between concern and indifference seemed to be called for. Human reactions vary according to circumstance: within some families, the non-appearance of an individual member might arouse no anxiety whatever for an entire day, but this was a category to which people like the Brents had never belonged. Bearing this in mind, I took the decision which had been stealing up on me for the past hour. Giving the pair of them a rallying grin which ate into my facial muscles, I said offhandedly, 'The sensible thing is to contact the authorities. With luck, your mother might get a lift home at public expense.'

Debbie gave a quick nod. Carol's eyes widened.

CHAPTER TWO

The duty sergeant sounded not displeased to have something to deal with on a Sunday afternoon.

'How long, sir? About three hours and a half? Sounds quite a walker, your wife. Most likely she's met up with someone unexpectedly, gone in somewhere, lost count of the time. Happens more often than you might think.'

'I'm sure you're right.' I spoke with the calm rationality proper to a citizen alive to his rights but aware of his duties. 'It's not typical of her, but then of course it's a beautiful day and she may have . . .' I forgot how I had planned to finish the sentence, so I abandoned it. The sergeant proceeded smoothly.

'Can you give me a description, sir? In case one of our chaps happens to spot her.'

'I'm not sure what she was wearing. I didn't actually see

her go out. She might—'

'Yellow blouse,' Debbie hissed at my elbow, 'and white skirt.'

'Apparently she—'

'Yes, sir, I heard that. Personal features? Dark or fair?'

'Well, she's . . .'

'Oh Dad.' Debbie wrested the receiver from me. 'This,' she announced clearly, 'is Mrs Brent's daughter speaking. You want to know what my mother looks like? She's about average height, fair, rather plump . . . Got that? I'm fairly sure about the blouse and skirt. She had them on before I left this morning, and I doubt if she'd have bothered to change. Age?' She squinted at me.

'Forty-four,' I contributed. 'But, Debbie—'

'She's forty-four. No, she doesn't wear specs. That all you need? I'll pass you back to my father.'

I took the receiver. 'Look,' I said, 'My daughter—'

'I'll alert the patrols, Mr Brent, around the district. But I think you'll find she'll show up before long. She'll have been unavoidably delayed somewhere, you mark my words.'

'I hope you're right, but—'

'Let us know, won't you, when she gets back?'

'Yes,' I said hesitantly. 'We'll certainly do that.'

Cradling the receiver, I turned to the girls who were watching expectantly. Carol was biting her lower lip. My attempt at a satisfied tone was less than a triumph. 'If anything had happened,' I told them, placing a hand on Carol's shoulder, 'he'd have heard about it. He didn't know anything, which is a good sign. We agreed there's some simple explanation and she'll be home quite soon. But I think you misled him a little, Debbie. Your description was a shade off-beam.'

'No, it wasn't,' she protested.

'Mousy-brown, I'd call your mother's hair. And I certainly wouldn't say she was plump.'

'What else would you call her?' She glanced at Carol, who nodded.

'Of course she's plump, Dad.'

I shrugged. 'Obviously my conception of a slim build is old-hat. We won't argue about it. The chief thing is to have her back. What time is it now?' With a certain fearfulness we all consulted our wrists. 'Just after two,' I said, cramming buoyancy into the syllables. 'I suppose it's really not that late. Plenty of families don't eat till three on a Sunday.'

'Other families,' Debbie said quietly.

'One has to allow for the unpremeditated, sweetheart. It's not an immutable law that everyone gets back sharp to time. What if she tripped and cut her leg open? She could be having attention in a house that's not on the phone . . .'

'She'd get a message to us somehow,' Carol declared. She sounded close to tears.

'Tell you what.' They both glanced up. 'I'll get the car out and drive around the streets, cover her favourite routes — how's that?'

'I'll come too,' they said in unison.

'One of us had better stay, in case she comes back another way and gets here first.'

'Carol can stay.'

'I want to go with Dad.'

'Toss for it.' I spun a coin. Debbie called wrongly and turned away with drooped shoulders.

'Go on,' she said. 'Be quick.'

'There!' said Carol for the fourth time.

The figure she was pointing to proved at closer range to belong to a woman in her sixties, gaunt-featured and walking with a limp. Accelerating, I took the next turning to the left, aware of the discouraged huddle of Carol's body at my side. I was beginning to question the

reluctance of women in the Greater London area to
venture out alone: the area seemed to be swarming with
them, with or without accompanying pets. Carol said
forlornly, 'I wish we had a dog. He'd find her.'

'Not,' I pointed out, 'if she'd taken him along.'
Swinging the car into yet another unmetalled road, I tried
to avoid the worst of the craters while maintaining
observation. 'She may be home by now,' I added hope-
fully, picking up speed. 'We must have been out twenty
minutes.'

'Can't we phone from a callbox?'

'Tell me if you spot one.'

'Dad,' Carol said presently.

'Yes, love?'

'What exactly did Mum say before she went out?'

'Only that she was going for a stroll.'

'Nothing else? You're sure?'

'Darling, I was in the living-room and she spoke from
the hall. If she'd had anything particular to tell me, she'd
have stuck her head round the door.'

'So,' she said after another interval, 'you didn't actually
see her before she left?'

'No. What difference does it make?'

'I was just wondering if she seemed . . . upset or
anything.'

'She sounded perfectly normal. You saw her, didn't
you, at breakfast? She was fine then, to my recollection.'

'Nothing happened,' she persisted, 'after I went out?'

'Nothing, Carol. I promise. Look, who's that ahead, on
the far side? No, not her walk. I'll turn here. We'll go
back via Oak Avenue and the Park. What d'you bet me
she's home already?'

'Fifty pence,' Carol said promptly, 'that she is.'

'Easy winnings.' I breathed a silent prayer.

Walter Freebody's laundered BMW had been joined in
his driveway by Amelia's metallic-blue Renault. Evidently

she was home from the Barbican. As I drove into our own entrance, my heart sank once more: Debbie's face had appeared briefly at a downstairs window, a hand shading her eyes, before vanishing to reappear in the porch. She gazed towards us hopelessly as we clambered out. Carol uttered a soft moan.

'She's not back.'

The front garden path felt like sponge as I struggled across it, doing my best to assemble an expression of cool optimism. I dared not look at my watch. If it was before three o'clock, a voice kept twittering at me, there remained hope that it was just a mental lapse on Sara's part, an aberration induced by some diverting but innocent occurrence, something to be animatedly discussed over a late meal. If it had turned three . . . No rational basis existed for such a deadline. It merely represented a watermark, something to swim around. Debbie's first words were, 'It's twenty past three. Dad, where can she have got to?'

It was a lament, not a question. I slipped an arm about her, then the other around Carol as she joined us, sniffing audibly.

'Let's get back inside,' I suggested. 'Then we'll think of something.'

'Okay,' Debbie said huskily. 'We thought we'd just check, in case she'd dropped in. Sorry to have bothered you, Mrs Wheeler.' Dropping the phone, she stood staring down at it. 'I can't think of anyone else,' she muttered.

Through the doorway to the kitchen, the clock sneered its message: four o'clock precisely. Moving alongside her, I said, 'Can I have it for a moment, sweetheart?'

Listlessly she stepped aside. As I was dialling, I caught an exchange of glances between her and Carol, who looked like a child with anæmia. For their sakes, I made my voice firm and distinct. 'Duty sergeant, please.'

It was the same man, but this time there was a kinder note to his voice. I should have preferred his previous breeziness. 'Not back yet? That's tiresome for you, Mr. Brent. You've done some phoning around? And she's not with any of her usual . . . I see. Leave it with me, will you, for twenty minutes? I'll get back to you. What's your number?'

I told him, and rang off. 'I think they're going to make some enquiries. Debbie, how about a pot of tea? Soothe our nerves.' Her answering smile was no ghastlier, I guessed, than my own. She went into the kitchen, started rattling crockery.

For half an hour, Carol hadn't spoken. Impelling her gently through to the living-room, I sat with her in a pool of sunlight on the sofa and tried to think of half a dozen heartening words to say to her. The mid-afternoon glow from the window was like a sniggering off-stage chorus, mocking my speechlessness. I felt like drawing the curtains, blocking it out.

As Debbie reappeared with a loaded tray, the telephone shrilled in the hall.

'Well now, Mr Brent.' The duty sergeant's tone was more benevolent than ever, but noncommittal. 'Your wife doesn't seem to have been admitted to a local hospital or anything like that. We've no report of an accident. Tell me . . . does your wife make a habit of popping off like this, without saying what time —'

'If she did, I wouldn't be so mystified.' In deference to his patent desire to help, I kept my own voice in check. 'It's totally out of character. She'd never leave us in the dark. Either it's loss of memory, or . . .'

Deftly he plugged the gap. 'Or there's some explanation that hasn't dawned on you yet — but it will. That I'll guarantee. You know, we get plenty of enquiries like this, and ninety-nine times out of a hundred they turn out to be false alarms: you'd be amazed. Hang in there, Mr

Brent. She'll be home.'

'It's getting on for six hours.'

'What if she's taken it into her head to call on a relative? Impromptu visit. Her mother — '

'Her parents live in the Midlands.'

'She could have jumped on a train. If so, she might not have arrived yet, which would explain — '

'Sergeant, I know my wife. She wouldn't do such a thing.'

'Not in the ordinary way, maybe.'

'You're suggesting this morning was abnormal, for some reason?'

'Not this morning, necessarily. Look, sir, we shan't get far like this. Best thing I can do is to send someone around to have a chat with you and your daughter . . . do you have any other children?'

I mentioned Carol. She and Debbie were stationed tensely in the doorway of the living-room, hanging on my replies. 'Also we've a son, Peter, but he's away just now.'

'Oh yes?' The sergeant's voice became alert. 'Where's that?'

'Central France. He's on an exchange visit. My wife urged him to go and she hasn't been pining, if that's what you're thinking.'

After a brief silence he said, 'We'll have someone with you, Mr Brent, inside the hour. In the meantime, any information relating to your wife that the three of you can think of will be useful. And if possible, a recent photograph. We probably won't be needing all this, but it'll keep you occupied. I know how it is, waiting around.'

Thanking him, I hung up and turned to the girls. 'They're sending someone to ask a few questions. They might want a photo. Do we have one?'

Both of them looked as blank as I felt. We were that rarity, a family almost devoid of photographic records. Apart from shots of the three children as toddlers, Sara

and I had never bothered with the creation of a picture
album: Peter, in fact, was the only one of us who
possessed a camera of any sort, and the last time I could
recall his making use of it was when he was camping with
the Scouts at the age of thirteen and tried to capture his
tent-mates under canvas, with smudgy results. If he had
tried his hand since, I hadn't been around at the time.
Carol began shaking her head. Debbie, more positively,
made a move towards the stairs.

'There may be something in Pete's room,' she said,
without much conviction. 'I'll take a look.'

CHAPTER THREE

The manner of the detective-constable who arrived forty
minutes later was, to me, not soothing. He looked
nineteen, and seemed to be an adolescent mixture of
assertiveness and insecurity, a combination which gave a
rasping edge to his approach. After his fifth question, my
control snapped.

'I just don't see the point of these queries. I'm sorry, but
how do they help in tracing my wife?'

The girls looked at me in mute surprise. Evidently they
had seen nothing wayward in his line of enquiry. For his
part, he relaxed a little, as if my small outburst was more
in tune with what he had been trained to expect.

'You've reported your wife missing, Mr Brent. So we
need to have the picture, right? No point in your consulting us, otherwise.'

'That's right, Dad,' said Debbie anxiously.

'I can understand your wanting to know the essentials,
but why all this piffling detail? What does it matter how
she spent last week? It's where she is now that's
important.'

Leaning back in his chair, he crossed one check-trousered leg over the other and regarded me with a kind of whimsical appraisal that made me feel like a block of wood being attacked by a blunt saw. I had to look away. His entire personality grated on me. Sartorially, he seemed to have taken his cue from a cross-section of televised crime series. Open-necked lilac shirt, elasticated pigskin shoes . . . the general effect was to give a ludicrous connotation to the 'plain-clothes' tag which presumably clung to him. If my attitude was on the stuffy side, I didn't care. This might have been how the modern CID dressed for business: it didn't mean I had to like it.

'Of course,' he affirmed with an element of elder-brother forbearance, 'I agree that's the point at issue. But we won't reach it by pussyfooting around. Your wife's recent behaviour—'

'You talk as if she must have been showing symptoms of hysteria. She hasn't. She's been perfectly normal.'

Pointedly he turned from me to Debbie. 'Noticed anything about your mother? Absence of mind? Forgetfulness?'

She shook her head, eyeing me sidelong. 'I don't think she's been any different from usual.'

'You don't *think?*'

'I'm sure she hasn't.'

His gaze wandered on to Carol, whose headshake was wordless. Plainly she was near to breaking down. I hoped she could hang on until he was out of the house: if a crisis was imminent, I preferred to handle it alone. To distract his attention I said, 'I didn't catch your name.'

'Merton. Detective-Constable—'

'I got the rank,' I interrupted nastily. 'I'm sure you're acting in good faith, Merton, but it seems to me we're wasting precious minutes. Shouldn't we be organizing a search?'

'All in good time.' He hadn't appreciated my form of

address, but seemed disposed in the circumstances to meet it charitably. 'First things first. If it comes to a hunt, we need to know the sort of person we're looking for. Early days, though. She's not been missing long.'

'Only the whole day. It may be just a matter of hours, but to us —'

'You did say you'd phoned your wife's parents in Bromsgrove? And they've not seen her?'

'If they had, would I be answering your questions?'

'You're not answering them.'

I took a grip on myself. He was, after all, here to help. 'I spoke to her parents,' I said carefully, 'half an hour ago. They gave me a categorical assurance that she's not there. They haven't even heard from her for a week or more.'

'You're satisfied with that information?'

'What do you mean, exactly?'

His left hand made a circular gesture. 'It's not un-known for in-laws to close ranks at times of stress.'

'There hasn't *been* any stress. Everything's been ordinary and . . . and peaceful. We keep telling you.'

Dispassionately, Merton made a note. 'No harsh words, then, to drive her off. Let's talk about other possible worries. Health?'

'She's in great shape.'

'Are you saying that because you know, or from what she's told you?'

I took a heavy breath. 'Both, if you like. When some-body bounces around like a five-year-old, you don't have to ask if she's feeling low.'

'Finance?' The Manual of Procedure, missing persons, section one, had clearly made an impression on Merton at police college. 'Any cash problems, that you know of?'

'There's plenty in her bank account. Yes, I do know that for a fact. She left her statement lying around just the other day: I don't snoop on her, but I happened to see it. Besides . . .'

'Yes, Mr Brent?'

'If you knew my wife, you'd realize how alien it would be to her nature to overspend.'

'I'm starting to know your wife,' he said drily.

Stifling a retort, I awaited his next question. It arrived on cue. 'Can I ask what you do for a living? Professional man, I take it?'

'I run a small business of my own. Road haulage.'

'Doing okay?'

'Fair to promising.'

'Keeps you busy, I dare say. Out a good deal?'

'During the week, naturally.'

'Does your wife help?'

'You mean, with office work? No, I keep all that separate. I operate from premises in Wimbledon. Sara — my wife stays at home and sees to everything here.'

Passing a couple of fingertips down his left cheek, as if prospecting for latent bristle, Merton looked contemplatively around the room. 'Not that big a house, is it? Does she find enough to keep her active?'

'She's never complained of under-occupation.'

He twitched a shoulder. He was full of mannerisms, mostly of the kind which are cultivated as acceptable responses to the half-anticipated. 'People,' he remarked with a secret smile, 'do occasionally get bored. It's a point one shouldn't overlook.'

I was collecting more breath when Debbie intervened. 'My mother,' she said in a dignified way, 'leads a very full life. Apart from running the house, she does work of her own. That takes up a fair slice of her time.'

Merton showed interest. 'What kind of work?'

'Home dressmaking. She makes up outfits for people, to order. She's quite good. Charges a fair price.'

'Great,' said Merton, his interest waning. 'Where does she find her customers?'

'Sometimes she advertises in the local paper. But

mainly it's by word of mouth. One client gives her name
to another.'

'Can any of this,' I asked, 'have any possible bearing on
my wife's disappearance? Time seems to be ticking past
while we —'

Abruptly Merton rose to his feet. 'I'd like to take a look
in one or two of the rooms,' he announced. 'Perhaps
you'll show me around, Mr Brent. Can we make a start
upstairs?'

He stood surveying the twin beds with their pink and
silver coverlets, natural pine side-tables, quilted
headpieces. Presently, with a deliberate movement, he
gave the door a shove so that it closed with a click, leaving
us closeted together in an atmosphere of curled feathers
and linen. He turned his attention to me.

'While we're up here by ourselves, there's something
else I want to ask.'

'What is it?'

Sauntering across to the built-in dressing-table, he
carried out an idle inspection of its array of cosmetic
containers. Without turning, he said, 'On a personal
basis, how have things been between you and your wife?'

'Fine.' Although it invaded more intimate ground, the
question seemed to me more apposite than most of his
others. There was less resentment in my answer.

'No marital difficulties?'

'None whatever.'

'The reason I'm asking —'

'Yes, I understand the reason, and I can put an end to
any speculation on that score.' My ability at this moment
to construct such a rounded sentence caused me vague
surprise.

He turned to study me in a way that, had I allowed
myself, I could have found offensive. 'Your wife's a few
years older than yourself, I think you said?'

'Four, to be accurate. But that's never mattered. No problem.'

'You've total confidence in each other?'

'I've done my best to make that clear.'

His gaze left me, skidded to the window. 'Right you are,' he said briskly. 'One or two further questions, if you'll bear with me. I'm assuming you've searched the house?'

'Ground-floor to roof.'

'Garden? That's a sizeable plot you've got out there.'

'The girls have scoured every inch. You can't think we'd have overlooked such an obvious—'

'We prefer to ask,' he said briefly. 'People are funny sometimes. You wouldn't believe.' Redirecting his attention to the bedroom, he stood assessing the furniture for a few moments before making purposefully for the door. 'This dressmaking of your wife's . . . does she use a separate room?'

'Yes. That door across the landing.' I showed him inside. On the worktable, Sara's electric sewing-machine stood guard over a length of gaudy material whose ultimate shape and purpose could only be guessed at; the job appeared to be less than half-finished. Having pondered it for a while, Merton went methodically around the room, opening drawers and cupboards, finding nothing that seemed to intrigue him. Going to the window, he peered out at the street and grunted.

'Nice outlook from both sides. Tell us about your daughters, Mr Brent. The younger one's about to take her O-levels, right? What does her sister do?'

'Debbie's a library assistant in the town.'

'And you've also a son, I believe. Holidaying on the Riviera.'

'Lyons. He's staying with a pen-friend.'

'He the oldest?'

'No. Seventeen.'

Merton's gaze through the panes became rapt. Presently he said, 'He and your wife . . . would they be pretty close?'

'Like most mothers and sons,' I said patiently. 'But he's been away from home several times before without causing her to distintegrate. If she'd been desperate to talk to him, she only had to lift the phone. She'd hardly make a sudden wild dash to France to see him. Anyhow, she couldn't.'

'Why not?'

'She hasn't a passport. Never wanted to travel abroad.'

A shadow of chagrin crossed Merton's face. 'I was about to mention that. What's the position, then, about a photograph?'

'Debbie was searching. I'll ask her if she had any luck.'

Downstairs, Debbie was sitting on the sofa with Carol sprawled across her lap, face down. Debbie was stroking her hair. Merton said importantly, 'She should be in bed with a sedative.'

I looked helplessly at Debbie. 'Do we have anything like that?'

'We'd have to phone Dr Ellis. But she doesn't —'

Carol's tear-streaked face came up with a jerk. 'I'm not going to bed,' she said tonelessly.

'We'll wake you if . . .'

'I'm staying here.' Regaining an upright position, she mopped her eyes, thrust back her dark hair with defiant movements of both hands. Debbie gave me a doubtful glance.

I lifted my shoulders. 'Whatever you say, darling. Debbie, we were wondering about a photo. Did you manage to track one down?'

She nodded at the circular table near the glazed doors. 'Over there.'

Merton went and picked it up. 'Recent?' he asked, studying the print.

'My brother took it at Christmas.'

I said, 'I don't remember.'

'He had one shot left on the film, so he —'

Merton was beckoning to me. 'Reasonable likeness, Mr Brent, would you say?'

I joined him at the table. The print lay on the polished inlaid surface with Merton's thumb on the edge of it: presently I became aware that the thumb was tap-tapping with evident restiveness. His voice boomed suddenly in my ear. 'Well? Is it or isn't it?'

Still looking, I said, 'I think my daughter's made a mistake, actually. This isn't my wife.'

CHAPTER FOUR

'Not your wife? Who is it, then?'

'I've no idea.' I turned to Debbie. 'Sweetheart, you seem to have picked up the wrong snap. Where did you get it?'

'From Pete's room, of course.' With a rallying squeeze of Carol's arm, she jumped up and came across. After a glance at the print she looked up questioningly into my face. 'What do you mean, the wrong one?'

I blinked back at her. 'Can't you see? That's not Mum. It's somebody else.'

She stared down at it again. 'It's Mum,' she said, her voice higher than usual and cracking a little. 'You know it is.'

'Now wait a bit.' Merton's fist moved in once more, captured the print, lifted it from the table. 'We all know the camera can lie, but let's not get hysterical about this. Maybe it's a poor likeness, but if it's something we can use . . .'

'It's not a question of a likeness,' I explained. 'There's

just no resemblance to my wife.'

'How can you say that, Dad? It's exactly like her.'

Merton studied us both in turn. 'Six months,' he remarked. 'I guess people *can* change out of recognition in that time. But you — ' he addressed Debbie ' — you seem convinced it's a fair copy of your mother as she is now. Your father doesn't agree. Who's right?'

'It's almost a perfect —'

'I'm afraid,' I interrupted tetchily, 'the point isn't worth discussing. Sorry, Debbie, but you're too upset to be thinking straight. That woman there, whoever she is, simply doesn't match up with your mother in any respect. She might be around the same age, but that's as far as it goes. Take another look.'

'I don't have to,' she objected. Nevertheless she examined the print again, before nodding decisively. 'That's Mum — large as life. I don't know how you can say it's not.'

She appealed to me with her eyes. Silence infested the room. Reversing the print, Merton glanced at the back, which I could see was blank, and then propped it face-upward at an angle against the cut-glass fruit dish on the table's centre. He stood off to divide his survey between it and the pair of us. From the sofa, there was a stir as Carol came to her feet and shuffled over. She stood staring speechlessly at the two-dimensional face in black and white against a neutral background. Merton watched her expectantly.

'What do you say, Carol? Is it recognizably your mother, or not?'

She gave a small sniff and a gulp. 'That's her,' she said. 'You couldn't ask for a better likeness.'

If I had hoped for an antidote to the Merton image in the form of his superior officer, I was disappointed. Detective-Inspector Richard Sinclair, as he took pains to introduce himself, elocuting each syllable with a precision that suggested he had run into trouble previously for identity-concealment, was no more visually presentable than his subordinate. A thin, stained, navy-blue blazer covered the upper part of him loosely; his legs were hidden beneath his desk, but there seemed no reason to suppose that they had fared any better when he dressed that morning. His manner was ambivalent. And the same was true of his speech: despite his careful diction, it was obvious that fundamentally he was poorly-spoken and perhaps ill-educated. Although I hope I'm no snob about such things, I happen to believe that in certain situations they can tilt the balance. A detective of the old school, all culture and consideration, might have coaxed more out of me that evening.

'How do *you* explain it?' he demanded for the third time.

'I tell you, I can't. An explanation doesn't exist.'

'Claptrap.'

He stood up and prowled. His trousers were beige, baggy and frayed at the pockets. His first-floor room at the police station faced west, with the result that the plummeting sun was shooting its rays straight against the pastel-green interior wall and building the temperature to intolerable heights, adding to my sensation of physical sickness. He spun about. 'I've been a few years in the Force, Mr Brent. I've yet to encounter a puzzle that couldn't be answered. Professional frustration — that's something else. Inability to collect evidence, get a conviction. But inexplicable mystery . . . That, let me tell you, is for the fiction scribblers. *That's* what doesn't exist.'

Following his movements back to his chair, I said, 'Who's arguing? All I meant was, I'm not capable of clarifying the matter. I'm hoping you can. But all you seem to be doing is asking interminable questions. When are you going to actually start looking for my wife?'

He offered no reply. Unlike Merton, who looked ill-nourished, he had a heavily-fleshed face with a dense colour, surmounted by close-packed ringlets of black hair touched with silver-grey at the temples. For a large man, he had small ears. He seemed about the same age as myself, or possibly a year or two older. These details I recorded abstractedly, as if some unfrozen part of me felt that they mattered.

'You look shagged,' Sinclair said abruptly.

'You'd be worn out, after a day like I've had.'

'Fairly used to them, though, aren't you? I'd have thought you'd take them in your stride by now.'

My frown was not a conventional response: I was struggling to pinpoint his meaning. 'What makes you say that?'

He shrugged massively. 'When a man like you, Mr Brent, fails to recognize his own wife from a perfectly good snapshot, it doesn't take genius to conclude that he's been under strain for a while. Does it now?'

I delayed my reply until I was sure I had it right. 'In the first place, there's been no stress until today. That's point one. Point two is, the reason I can't identify that photograph is quite simply that it's *not* my wife. After twenty years of marriage, I feel I should know.'

He passed me a cigarette, stuck one between his own lips and lit up for both of us. As the smoke coiled and merged, he said mildly, 'And your two daughters? They seem intelligent. Don't they know their own mother?'

'Of course they do.'

'In that case—'

'Oh, look. They're both distraught and confused. My wife vanishing like this has flung them off balance. Can you blame them for squiffy vision?'

Thoughtfully he inhaled. 'Goes a little beyond that, doesn't it? According to you, the woman in the photo can't possibly be mistaken for your wife.'

I leaned forward. 'Put it this way. You've got two film actresses — okay? Both the same height, both red-haired, both around thirty. Superficially they've a lot in common. But what happens if you shoot a film with one of them and bill it as starring the other? An outcry, that's what. The cinema public aren't going to be fooled. They can spot the difference at a glance.'

Sinclair scowled up at the drifting smoke. 'Begging the question, aren't we? That scenario may support your argument. Equally, it bears out what your daughters are saying. Why should they be fooled, either?' He paused. 'And it's not just them, I might add.'

In the act of flicking ash, I stayed my hand. 'What's that?'

'We showed the photograph to your neighbours. They identified it.'

'As my wife?'

He nodded, keeping me under survey.

I put fingers to my collar, trying to detach it from overheated flesh. 'Which neighbours?'

'Both sides.' He consulted a notepad at his elbow. 'Mr Alfred Montgomery. Mr and Mrs Walter Freeman — Freebody. They all agreed with your daughters.'

The room made a threatening movement. Breathing hard, I sat straighter in my chair, unobtrusively gripping the armrests: I wanted no more cracks from Sinclair about strain and stress.

'First,' I suggested, 'let's take old Mr Montgomery. Nice enough chap, but his wife died years ago and he's been virtually a recluse ever since. He's deaf, and I dare say his eyesight isn't what it was. I doubt if he's even seen my wife for quite a while. If he identified the photo, it must have been from memory — and a shaky one at that.'

Sinclair retained his neutrality of tone. 'My information is, he said "That's her" without hesitation.'

'I expect he just wanted to get your chap off his
doorstep. As for the Freebodys, that's rather more
puzzling, I'll admit, but not unaccountable. The fact that
we're neighbours is neither here nor there. Candidly,
we've never cared for them much. They're social
climbers. So we've always tended to keep out of their way,
and besides this, Inspector, my wife doesn't normally
leave the house a great deal, anyway. Did Constable
Merton tell you? She does home dressmaking, which
keeps her indoors an awful lot. I doubt if the Freebodys
have clapped eyes on her more than twice in the past
twelve months.'

'Surely she goes shopping occasionally?'

'Most of the stuff we need, the girls bring in. Sara
detests shops.'

'What does she do for exercise?'

'Gardening. We've nearly half an acre. She spends
hours out there, pottering around.'

Sinclair screwed up his eyes. 'Another recluse,' he said
edgily, 'like your Mr Montgomery?'

'Don't twist my words. All I'm saying is, my wife's a
home-loving type who's not interested in social high-
flying. Long ago the Freebodys sniffed this out for
themselves and lost interest in us. Therefore, if neither of
them is really certain just what my wife looks like, I can't
pretend to be staggered.'

Rising slowly, Sinclair performed another prowl which
ended at the window. 'In that case, why would both of
them be prepared to identify her from an amateur
snapshot?'

'Put yourself in their place. A policeman knocks and
asks whether they recognize their next-door neighbour
from a photograph. "We wouldn't like to say." Is this
what they're going to answer? Make themselves look
idiots? Much easier to reply, "Yes, that's Mrs Brent," and
be done with it.'

Smoke from his cigarette jetted against the glass. 'On the other hand, why should they care? If they're the sort of people you describe, they'd hardly mind being vague about someone they've lived alongside for several years. On the contrary. My guess is, they'd be rather pleased with themselves.'

I gestured. 'That's a matter of opinion.'

'Granted.' Making a second return to the desk, he leaned bulky thighs against its rim. 'And what we in the CID deal with, as you'll know from your crime fiction intake, are facts, not opinions. Hard evidence. Anything else is moonshine.'

I stared up at him. 'Why do you keep harping on fiction?'

'Do I?'

'You seem to be implying that I'm an addict of cheap thrillers. I'm not. Personally, I enjoy a good biography.'

'Thrillers,' he remarked inconsequentially, 'don't come cheap, these days.'

I moved painfully in my chair. When I first took occupation, its seat had been padded leather: in the course of the interview it had become unyielding metal, complete with spikes, and this was having an effect on my ability to concentrate. There were things I wanted to say, logic-packed arguments I yearned to present; but it was all too much trouble. Whatever I said, Sinclair seemed to have an answer to. Or, more jarringly, a half-answer: a stop-volley into the forecourt, leaving me sprinting to make ground. Sinclair was looking out at the street below. Taking advantage of the back of his head, I snatched a glance at my watch.

Nine-thirty. I had been here an hour and three-quarters, and there was no sign that Sinclair wanted to be rid of me. The girls would be going off their heads. Fury added itself to my inner turmoil. As if receiving the vibrations, he turned back.

'Feeling ragged at the edges, Mr Brent?'

'How would you feel?'

'If my wife had gone missing . . .' His eyes went a little glassy. 'Know what I'd be doing? I'd be co-operating like crazy with the investigating authority. Common sense, isn't it? Second nature, you might say, to any law-abiding inhabitant. Assuming, that is, he was anxious for enquiries to succeed.'

Heaving himself clear of the desk's support, he moved lazily around until he was in position to fall into his own chair, which accepted him with a brief screech of castors. He sat back, pulled lengthily on the remaining inch of his cigarette before grinding it to fragments in a chipped saucer already black with ash. Dusting his thick fingers, he gazed at a framed certificate attached to the wall alongside the window. His body became still. The room's silence made space for exterior noises: the zoom of an engine, the clash of heels on paving.

'Just what,' I enquired softly, 'are you asking me to do? Make a false identification of a photograph—just to please you?'

His eyes flicked back. 'Please *me*? You've an odd way of looking at things, Mr Brent. It's you we're trying to satisfy. We'd love to get your wife back for you.'

'Then why don't you concentrate on that?'

'Who are we looking for?'

I waited a moment. 'You're asking me? You seem convinced it's the woman in that photo.'

'And you're doing your level best to persuade us it's not.'

'Does it really matter? Good God, there can't be that many forty-four-year-old brown-haired women wandering around lost at any given time. All you need do—'

'Care for a small bet on that?'

I glared at him in silence.

'It might surprise you,' he elaborated, 'to learn the

precise figure relating to . . . Excuse me. What colour hair did you say?'

'Brown. Brownish.'

'Your wife's fair, according to your daughters.'

I brandished an arm. 'Fairish, brownish. What's the difference?'

'If you can't make the distinction,' he said deliberately, 'then I don't wonder you have trouble with photographs. Is she fair-skinned, your wife?'

'You could say so.'

'You're not sure?'

'You wouldn't call her swarthy,' I said irritably.

'What would you call me?'

'Don't tempt me.'

'Go ahead. Describe me.'

'You're on the dark side, of course. But all this,' I added, hearing my voice soar, 'is entirely irrelevant. It has nothing to do with colour-blindness. As far as that snapshot is concerned, it's the shape of the face, the eyes—everything. How do you define the variations between features? You just know them when you see them.'

'Quite,' he said, with emphasis.

'Which takes us back to square one. Don't tell me. I'm sick of being *told*. I don't know how much more of this I can stand.'

Sinclair looked reflective. 'You don't have to put yourself through the hoop.'

'How true. All I need do is say to you, *Oh, I'm wrong—of course that's my wife in the photograph.* Then all you need do is start fanning out to look for her, and I could have a rest from your questions. Easy. Why didn't I think of that?'

'We're looking for her, Mr Brent. Right now.'

'Who is "her"? Nobody seems to know, do they?'

'Wrong. Everyone seems to know, except you.'

Outside, a car's motor screamed briefly, subsided as

the vehicle reached the junction, set up another howl, lost itself in distance. The wince that had frozen on Sinclair's face thawed slowly to leave the flat, featureless expanse I had been looking at since entering the room. I felt like trampling over it, leaving footprints.

'If I could have another word with my daughters . . .'

'You think that would achieve anything?'

Silence stretched itself like Polythene sheeting between us.

'How long do you intend keeping me here?'

'You're not being kept. If you want to leave, I can't stop you.'

Stiffly I rose. 'Thanks,' I said with a touch of bitterness, 'for making it so clear from the outset. Before I go, you're sure there's no other suspect information I can feed you? False history, phoney credentials . . . nothing of that sort?'

'You might just confirm—' he bent forward, riffling through the sheets of paper on his desk—'the Bromsgrove address of your in-laws. Vicarage Court, Kidderminster Lane. That right?'

'I'll go along with that.' At the door, I paused. 'There's just one thing I should perhaps warn you about.'

Sinclair looked up from his blotter. 'What might that be?'

'If you're hoping for an identification of the photo from my wife's parents, you could be in for a letdown. Both of them are practically blind.'

CHAPTER FIVE

When I arrived back, the girls were in the living-room. Debbie was at the sliding doors, staring into the twilit garden. Carol sat in a bunched attitude on the sofa, as though she hadn't stirred since my departure. The television picture was turned on, soundless. Debbie whirled as I came in. I gestured at the set.

'Do we need that?'

'We were waiting for the news.'

'Why?'

'There might be something . . .' Her words trailed away. She stood regarding me in a dumbly enquiring manner that robbed me of speech. I turned to Carol.

Her eyes were shut, but I had the feeling she had been looking at me in the way that she used to at the age of about six, at bedtime, when she was clinging tenaciously to the hope that by keeping still and looking small she might contrive to remain unnoticed for an extra twenty minutes. Ten years on, she didn't look noticeably older. Swallowing hard, I went to the TV set and snapped it off.

'There won't be anything. We'd have heard.'

The elimination of the screen's flickering glow seemed to haul a thick curtain across the room. Moving past me, Debbie switched on the lights, then stayed by the wall, eyeing her sister. I said, 'Have you eaten at all?'

'Coffee and biscuits. We couldn't face a lot.'

'Try not to neglect yourselves,' I said uselessly.

Debbie fingered the switches. 'Did they tell you anything?'

'Only that I'm barmy, or a liar.' In an attempt to take the sting out of the words, I added, 'You phoned Pete?'

'I got through, but he wasn't there. Apparently he and Françoise and a couple of her friends have gone off camping for a few days.'

I moaned softly. 'Can't they be contacted?'

'They're not sure where they've gone.'

'Did you ask Madame Bardeau to notify the gendarmerie?'

Doubt showed in Debbie's face. 'I didn't say anything about Mum. Thought I'd wait till you got back, in case I caused a fuss for nothing. Dad . . .'

I gave her my full attention. 'Yes, Deborah?'

She flinched perceptibly. The last time I had used her proper name was when, as a third-former, she had brought home an inexcusably atrocious report for the term and had required shaking up. 'What did they say,' she continued falteringly, 'at the police station? About the photo?'

Seating myself on a footstool, I lit my fifth cigarette of the day. 'Seems they showed it to the Freebodys, and old Monty next door.'

She waited. 'And?'

'They all agreed with you and Carol.'

She studied me intently. 'But you still say it's a rotten likeness?'

I made a business of stowing my lighter. 'I think,' I said slowly, 'there's one thing we should get absolutely clear. As far as I'm concerned, there's only one statement to be made about the person in that photograph: she's a stranger to me. It's not my wife; it's not your mother. Can I speak any plainer?'

A sob came from Carol. She buried her face in a sofa cushion.

'Now you've upset her again.' Debbie went and sat beside her, held her shoulders. 'You don't have to keep harping. The chief thing is, the police have at least got a photo of sorts, and if they can use it to help trace Mum, that's all that matters, surely?'

'But this is just my point. How can they—'

I stopped. Manifestly it was futile. No form of words I could devise would convey the message. 'There's only one thing for it,' I resumed presently. 'Forget about the snapshot. Concentrate on essentials. For some reason, your mother went out this morning and hasn't come back—let's take it from there. You first, Debbie. How did she seem at breakfast? Notice anything unusual about her?'

Vigorously she shook her head. 'Merton asked me that. She was just like she always is.'

'Talkative?'

'Quite chatty. We were discussing the Carnival Fête next Saturday. She said she was going to contribute some flowers from the garden for one of the floats, and make a couple of costumes for the mermaids. Apparently one of the organizers phoned and asked her. She was a bit nervous about it. The stitching—'

I grasped at the straw. 'You don't think it could have been preying on her mind?'

'Oh, Dad. She wasn't taking it that seriously. It just came up in conversation, that's all. That was before you came down and started on about the price of diesel fuel.'

'Which took us on to the cost of living generally,' I said, scanning back. 'Your mother didn't contribute much to that debate—am I right?'

'No. While we were setting the world to rights, she went out to the garden and picked some gladioli. She was putting them in vases for the rest of breakfast.'

'After the meal, I brought the newspapers in here and got immersed. Next thing I heard was your mother's announcement that she was off. Let me ask you something, Debbie. After I left the kitchen, did anything happen?'

'Like what?'

'Did either you or Carol have words with her, of any kind?'

'Of course not! It's the first thing I'd have mentioned. I'll tell you just what happened. Carol reminded us she was going round to help the curate, and then I said I'd be spending the whole morning with Maureen and Brenda. So Mum said, *In that case, I'll do an hour on those dratted costumes and then get some fresh air before lunch. Try not to be late.*'

'She said that?'

'More or less. I don't recall the exact words.'

'She didn't ask what you'd be doing with Maureen and Brenda?'

Debbie looked mystified. 'Why should she? She knows we're writing a play together.'

'And she didn't seem upset that you were going off for the morning?'

'She was all for it. *That's right*, she said, *make use of the weekend, don't fritter it away.* Honestly, Dad, there wasn't any hassle. Not with me, at any rate.'

Both of us looked speculatively at Carol, whose face had re-emerged. Although she had seemed to be barely listening, her head now began to shake. In a choked voice she said, 'She was quite good-tempered. Right up until I left.'

Debbie glanced back at me. 'How about you? You're positive you didn't *say* anything to her?'

On the verge of indignantly refuting the suggestion, I hesitated. Debbie was quick to pounce. 'You did say something. What was it?'

The reason for my hesitation was hard to define. Sara and I were not in the habit of arguing—I couldn't recall so much as an exchange of sharp words—and it seemed improbable that this morning had been any different. The plain fact was, however, that I was utterly unable to bring to mind in detail the period between the end of breakfast and the moment when Sara had called to me through the door; a clear denial therefore was something I felt unjustified in giving. 'If I did,' I compromised, 'it was so harmless that it's gone out of my head.'

'Out of yours, perhaps. What if Mum took it to heart?'

'That's ridiculous. What could I have said? I wasn't feeling strongly about anything in particular.'

'Well, maybe it's *because* you didn't say anything. She

could have felt neglected.'

'Does that sound like your mother?'

'It's not like her to vanish, either.' Debbie spoke with a catch in her throat.

'We shan't get anywhere like this.' At the back of my mind I was still uneasy: I should have liked to be able to formulate a mental picture of that after-breakfast period. 'We've got to decide,' I went on with an attempt at firmness, 'on the best immediate course of action. First of all, I think Carol should go upstairs to bed.'

She came out with a low wail. 'I'm staying down here.'

'Me too, Dad. There's no point in either of us trying to sleep.'

'You ought to have some tablets, the pair of you. Help you rest.'

'Rest!'

'No sense in battering yourself, sweetheart. The police are involved now. There's not much we can do except wait. They'll find her, don't you worry.' My words sounded so hollow that I continued hurriedly, 'Tell you what. I'll slip next door, see if Mrs Freebody has anything for insomnia. She's the type that might. You two wait here, huh? Listen out for the phone.'

I left before either of them could reply. It was with a slightly shamefaced sense of release that I regained the warm June dusk of the street, impassive under the star-light. Instead of turning into the Freebodys' driveway I crossed the road and walked to the corner, turned there, took the secondary street for a few hundred yards until I reached Welling Avenue. Number 16: 'Secateur'. The lunatic house-name had stuck in my memory from the telephone directory earlier in the day. It was a large, double-fronted house, set well back, with a vast former window dominating its roof and, ironically, a faintly ramshackle look about its lawns and flowerbeds. My pressure on the doorbell was answered by a watery light

inside the hall, followed by the shooting of innumerable
bolts, the creation of a slim gap between door and frame,
the semi-appearance of a male face.

'Who is it?'

'Ralph Brent. Sara Brent's husband. You remember I
called—'

'Hah. Yes.' Chains rattled. The broadened fissure
showed me a short, scrawny, peppery-looking man of
about sixty with zinc hair, combed very straight. He wore
square-rimmed spectacles which he now removed to
examine me. 'Wife got back all right, did she? Not
poorly, I hope?'

'She hasn't shown up, I'm afraid.'

'Oh dear. Oh dear me. I'm very sorry to—'

'Who is it, Brian?'

'Sara Brent's husband, dear. She's gone missing,
apparently.'

'What? Sara?' Mrs Peterson advanced into view. In
contrast to her husband she was built on a generous scale,
with rounded cheeks under a mass of toppling coppery
hair; and by disposition she seemed more placid,
although she was showing concern. 'Missing?' she
repeated, studying me closely. 'Since when? Do come
inside, Mr Brent. We've not met, have we? Brian, don't
keep people on the doorstep. How worrying for you.
When was it that she—?'

'This morning. She went for a walk and hasn't come
back.'

Pursuing them through to a vividly-lit, untidy living-
room at the rear of the house, I felt suddenly emotional.
Theirs was the first genuinely sympathetic reaction I had
met, so far, and it had caught me unprepared. When Mrs
Peterson impelled me down into a sling-backed chair, I
offered no resistance. 'Forgive me,' I said, 'for troubling
you at this hour—but there's something I'm rather
anxious to ask you.'

'Anything we can do, old man, to help. Any single thing.' Peterson gave his wife a glare, as if challenging her to contradict him.

'Thanks. You know Sara pretty well, of course. You must have seen quite a bit of her . . .'

'We've been regularly *in touch*,' Mrs Peterson said amendingly. 'As you know, she's the very capable Membership Secretary of our Horticultural League, so we have to keep her posted on newcomers, departures, all that kind of thing. For her Files.' She glanced fondly at the hearthrug, where for the first time I noticed an elderly Labrador, sandy-beige, stretched out in an attitude of regal enjoyment alongside a tiny tortoiseshell cat which was curled in a slumbrous ball. 'Sara's always been a great help, Mr Brent, I can tell you. Hasn't she, Brian?'

'Fact.'

'But as for *knowing* her well . . . Actually, we've hardly met. The last time we saw her—oh, it must be all of five years. Just briefly, at the inaugural branch meeting. Ever since then, things seem to have rather conspired to keep us apart. Don't they, Brian?'

'Fact.'

'I know she was hoping to attend the last Annual General Meeting, but in the end something came up and she couldn't make it. That's how it's been, all along. So although we work in harness, you might say, we can't claim to be that familiar with her as a person, do you understand what I mean?'

'More of a postal and telephone relationship,' corroborated her husband.

I felt a deadness in the chest. 'Suppose you were shown a photo of my wife. Would you know her?'

Both of them sucked in their cheeks. 'To be truthful,' declared Mrs Peterson, stirring the Labrador with a toe, 'I couldn't say. I've just the dimmest recollection of your

wife's features, quite honestly. Medium height, is she?
Wears glasses?'

'High cheekbones?' ventured her husband.

I looked from one to the other in despair. 'You might
remember her colouring?'

Glassiness invaded their pupils. 'Fair?' hazarded Mrs
Peterson, at the same instant as her husband said, 'Dark?'

I climbed to my feet. 'I think I'm wasting your time.
You've been most kind and helpful and I mustn't impose
any more.' A thought hit me. 'Just one other thing. You
don't happen to keep a file record of the League's
activities?'

'Everything's tucked away,' Mrs Peterson confirmed
proudly.

'Press cuttings?'

'Of course. And our newsletters. The lot.'

'I was wondering . . .' They looked at me silently. 'It's a
great deal to ask, but would it be possible for us to have a
quick look through? There might conceivably be a picture
of my wife somewhere.'

Mrs. Peterson turned with alacrity towards a
mahogany bureau. 'You're welcome to see all we've got.'

While she brought it out by the armful, her husband
was conning me in a faintly puzzled way. 'You've no
photograph of Sara?'

'Only a rather unsatisfactory one.' I joined his wife at
the battered table on which she had spread the accumulated junk of years. She pushed across a cardboard file
secured with an elastic band.

'Press clippings. You might stumble across something
in there. Though I rather doubt . . .'

She became engrossed in another file containing letter-
headed documents. On her other side, Mr Peterson
helped himself to a selection and breathed heavily over
them. For a while, this and the crackle of paper were the
only sounds in the room.

Standing at the table, I became acutely conscious of fatigue in the small of my back, the calves of my legs. For ten hours I hadn't relaxed, had barely eaten, had drunk only coffee; the inevitable result was a sensation that I had been mangled between giant rocks and then hung out to bleach. I forced myself to concentrate. The Press extracts were a mass of trivia, unillustrated items, of minimal fascination even to those involved. I was on the point of telling the Petersons to squander no more of their evening when a squeak of triumph made my heart jump. 'Found something?'

'I thought so.' Mrs Peterson was flourishing a newsletter. 'There was a group picture taken at the inaugural meeting. We used it in our first edition — look.'

She smoothed out the centrefold. Peering myopically, her husband whipped off his glasses, buffed the lenses and replaced them to peer again. 'Didn't reproduce too well,' he observed profoundly.

My own disappointment was too crippling to disguise. Intense analysis of the full-width rectangular smudge suggested that it comprised a two-tier line-up of human faces: beyond this, the detail had vanished irretrievably into the mists of over-inking. Beneath the smudge was a caption. Mrs Peterson spelled it out.

'*Left to right, front row: Mrs Franklin, hon. secretary; Mr Philip Coles, vice-chairman* . . .Here we are! *Mrs S. Brent, hon. membership secretary* . . .'

Her forefinger hovered.

'Might be anyone,' pronounced Peterson.

'Yes. I'm very much afraid you're right.' His wife sounded a little dashed. She turned to me. 'Not much help to you, I suppose?'

Summoning my resources, I hoisted a smile of gratitude across to her. 'Not really, but it was extremely kind of you to turn it up. You've no idea who took the original?'

They gave me their joint blank look. 'I can't imagine. Can you, dear?'

'Not a clue. We might ask Coles, he may possibly—'

'Leave it,' I told them. 'You've been more than helpful, as it is. And I must get back. I've left my daughters alone in the house.'

Mrs Peterson stood regarding me with a kind of puzzled compassion. 'Perhaps,' she murmured, 'you'll find Sara there, waiting for you. I do hope so.'

CHAPTER SIX

By-passing the street door, I walked round to the back of the house and looked cautiously through the sliding doors, still uncurtained. Carol was in her huddled position on the sofa. Debbie was staring at the TV. Retreating, I returned to the footway and went next door.

From the Georgian window of the front room I could hear the rattle of gunfire. It seemed to drown the door-bell, but after a few seconds the hall light came on as a prelude to the slightly dramatic self-exposure of Amelia Freebody in pink blouse and tight black pants above naked feet. Away from the house, I should never have known her. Although we had met briefly a few times, her appearance had never imprinted itself upon me: she tended to look different on each occasion. The thought occurred to me that, shown a black-and-white photograph of her face, I should have been taxed to put a name to it. On the tall side, and willowy, she wore her platinum hair this evening in softening waves about somewhat gaunt features, in relation to which the mouth was over-prominent. Her dark-circled eyes regarded me with an amused coolness.

'I've a feeling I should know you . . . Oh! Ralph! My

dear, I'm so sorry. These damn lights, they throw such
shadows. Sara got back?'

'Unfortunately, no.' Since we were barely on speaking
terms, let alone first-name ones, I refrained from echoing
her familiarity. 'Mind if I speak to you for a moment?'

'Come through. We're only watching the late movie.
That is, Walter's riveted to the screen while I do the
crossword. Darling—company. Switch that damn thing
off and fix some drinks.'

'Not for me.'

'Oh come on. You must need it. What with—'

The telephone interrupted her. She picked it up with a
grimace. 'Who? Oh—Deborah, love. Yes, your father's
here. Did you want a word?' With a pounding heart I
watched her expectantly, but she clung on to the receiver,
listening. Presently she said, 'I'll tell him. All right, my
dear, good night,' and hung up. 'Your daughter was
getting anxious about you.'

Guilt attacked me from all sides. 'We're all a bit on
edge,' I explained, glancing at the clock. I turned
apologetically towards Walter, clinking bottles at a
dispensary in the corner. 'Sorry to barge in on you like
this.'

He turned with a display of blinding teeth. 'What are
neighbours for? Try that, old son, and if you want more
ice, dig in. No news of Sara, then? Hell of a worry for you.
First we knew of it was when that copper called on us late
this afternoon, right, Amelia? The way he spoke, we got
the impression she'd just sort of gone off for the day. Are
they doing a full search?'

'I hope so.'

'They'll find her.' Amelia was keeping a strict check on
his bartending. 'Now they've got her picture . . .'

'That's really what I came in about. He showed you a
snapshot, didn't he?'

'The policeman? Yes, and asked us to confirm that it

was Sara.' She frowned. 'Bit odd, when you think about it.' She wrapped scarlet-dipped claws about a fizzing tumbler. 'Why should he want us to do that?'

'There was some disagreement,' I said, 'as to whether it was a good likeness or not.'

'I get it. Walter, could you jazz this up a bit? More of the basic, there's a love. Who disagreed?' she demanded, watching the neck of the bottle. 'I wouldn't have thought there could be much dispute about it.'

I pretended to take a sip of Scotch. 'You considered it was a good photo?'

'Perfectly clear print,' said Walter, bearing the revitalized glass back to his wife. 'No reason for any doubts.'

'This is what you told the officer?'

'More or less.' Suddenly he looked discomposed. 'Did we put our big feet right in it? We were assuming—'

'You're both quite satisfied that the picture was of my wife, Sara?'

They swapped glances. Walter said tentatively, 'You're telling us it wasn't?'

'Suppose I did. Would you be in a position to contradict me?'

'Hold it right there. I don't think I'm—'

'Wait a bit, Walter.' His wife quelled him with a claw. 'Listen to what Ralph's saying. Obviously it's important. That *wasn't* a photo of Sara—is that it?'

I looked at her steadily. 'I'd like your opinion.'

More glances flew around. Walter started a portentous clearing of the throat. First to the draw, Amelia said with a touch of frost, 'We've given our opinion already.'

'To the copper. What exactly did he do? Did he show you the print and ask whether you could say who it was?'

'He asked whether it was a recognisable snap of our neighbour.'

'To which your answer was "Yes"?'

'That's right, old man. And now you're here to tell us it was her sister?'

'She hasn't any sisters. I'm not here,' I said, hearing again the wobble in my voice, 'to make any concrete statements. All I want is information. To my mind, you see, it's not a picture of Sara at all; whereas the girls don't agree. This is where an impartial verdict would be useful.'

I studied them without hope. The upper part of Walter's face had gone into baffled creases. Amelia's, on the other hand, had smoothed over, become an enigmatically unmarked landscape. 'The girls think it *is* her?'

'They've no doubts.'

'Well, then?' She spread her talons.

'I'd still like to know what *you* think.'

'To be perfectly candid, Ralph,' she said after a pause, 'it's a teeny bit difficult for both of us. Not being what you might call intimate buddies of Sara . . .'

'What are you trying to say? That you're not completely sure what she looks like?'

'I'm trying to explain why one hesitates to be dogmatic. It's not as if Sara throws herself around. I mean, she's a shy person, let's face it.'

'Amelia's right, you know. What she's saying—'

'I understand what she's saying.' I deposited my full glass on a dresser. 'Don't get the idea I'm sniping at anyone. I just thought it was worth a check. Now you'll have to excuse me, I must get back to the girls. Which reminds me. Sleeping pills. Does either of you . . .'

'I'll see,' Amelia said curtly, and left the room.

'The trouble with urban living,' said Walter, fracturing an awkward silence, 'is this business of inter-communication. Maybe it's become kind of a cliché, but in an environment of walls and fences and motorized transport, when you get right down to it . . .'

I let him ramble on until his wife returned with a phial.

'I've had these a couple of years. They pack quite a punch, as I recall.' Her manner was distantly polite. 'How many do you want?'

'What's the dosage?'

'You'd better take the lot.' Handing them over, she walked past me and switched on the television. With her back to me as she studied the controls, she added, 'Let us know, won't you, when Sara shows up again? We wouldn't like to think she's missing if she's not.'

'Mrs A. Freebody, two capsules before retiring.' Debbie glanced up from the label. 'Will a couple be okay for Carol? I'm not sure if she counts as as adult.'

'I'd say she'll need at least two.'

'If she'll take them.'

'If necessary, we can dissolve them in coffee.'

'She's hardly drinking.'

I thrust fingers through my hair, which felt brittle, lifeless. 'We'll just have to do the best we can. How about you?'

'I don't want to take anything.'

'But you must rest. I'll keep awake, in case there's any . . . Besides, I've another call to make.'

'Who else is there to ring?'

Watching her movements about the kitchen as she reached for the coffee jar, fetched milk from the fridge, I felt as though I were seeing her for the first time for years. Just yesterday, it seemed, she had been a gawky fifteen-year-old with straight hair and a stutter. Overnight, she had hopped clear of adolescence into a state of womanhood, and suddenly it troubled me that I hadn't noticed. Most fathers, I told myself, went through a similar experience, if the advice columns were to be believed. Obsessed with the images of our small, dependent daughters, we shut our eyes to the fact that they were going to grow up and stop leaning on us. With adjusted vision, I could now see that Debbie was something of a teenage knockout. As though aware of my gaze upon her, she paused in the act of opening a milk carton, looked round and repeated her question. 'There's nobody, is there, we haven't contacted?'

'Only Pete.'

'Oh. Well, for the time being we can't. Madame Bardeau—'

'She must have a rough idea where they were heading. If she alerts the French police, they should be able to trace their camp site in a matter of hours.'

Debbie regarded me sombrely. 'You want them to do that?'

'It's not a question of wanting. If his mother is missing, Pete has a right to know.'

'Surely we could leave it till the morning? Mum could be back by then.'

'Of course she could.' The warmth of my response took some fuelling. 'In the meantime, though, I still think Pete should be notified. Let's have this coffee, get those capsules into Carol if we can: then I'll put a call through to Lyons.'

Debbie's gaze lingered for a second. 'You want to ask Pete about that photo.'

'Do you blame me?'

Fatigue trickled into her posture. 'I don't know, Dad. I honestly don't understand you. Why are you adopting this attitude towards that picture? Is it because Pete took it? Don't you approve of his photography?'

'Don't be absurd. I've tried to explain. It has nothing to do with the print, as such. It's the face it depicts. It's not Mum's. It's someone else's.'

Debbie broke down in tears. Rescuing the milk, I made a grab at her, but she eluded me and went to sit heavily on the stool by the cooker, her face averted. I felt the usual male clumsiness on such occasions. In addition, I was nervous about Carol, whose hearing was sharp; but Debbie, perhaps mindful of the danger, was making little noise. Most of her distress expressed itself in a heaving of the shoulders. I hated watching her, especially as I seemed to be the prime cause of the eruption. When she quietened a little, I passed her a handkerchief.

'Sweetheart . . .' To my own ears, I sounded like a clucking hen. 'You don't imagine I'm just trying to upset you?'

Wiping her eyes, she didn't reply.

'My sole concern is to help the police find her. To do that, they need an accurate description. All I'm saying . . .' I paused for a selection of words. 'What I'm arguing is that the snapshot we've given them could, in *my* view, be misleading. Therefore I'd like to ask Pete when and exactly where he took it. Okay?'

Blowing her nose, she handed back the handkerchief. 'You'd better phone, then. I'll be making the coffee.'

I got through to the Bardeau residence more promptly than I had reached anyone in the neighbourhood that day. In reply to the low-pitched '*Oui? Allo?*' of Françoise's mother, I made a fumbling start on the French phrases I had prepared; but she cut in smartly in irreproachable English. 'This is Mr Brent? Good evening, and how are you?'

'I'm very well.' In other circumstances I might have been stung by her calm and justified assumption that the conversation was better conducted in my language rather than hers. 'Sorry to trouble you at this hour, Madame Bardeau . . .'

'It's nothing. We're eating dinner—supper, you know? Outside, in the garden. It's fine weather here. The same in England?'

'The weather's been beautiful. But we have a problem, I'm afraid.'

'Problem? Your daughter telephoned me before, but she—'

'We didn't want to cause any fuss too soon.' Briefly I related what had occurred. She listened so attentively, without comment, that at one point I thought the connection had ben cut. 'Hullo? Still there?'

'Yes, I'm here. I'm so sorry, Mr Brent. How terrible for you all.' Her genuine sympathy resonated inside the earpiece. 'Peter should be told, of course. Unfortunately—'

'My daughter explained about the camping trip. What I'm wondering is, could you notify the gendarmerie and ask them to find them? Is that feasible?'

There was a short pause. 'Certainly we can ask,' said Madame Bardeau, sounding dubious. 'But they were not . . . Françoise didn't tell us their destination, you know?'

'You must have some idea.' The remark sounded testier than I had intended, but she seemed to take no offence.

'Young people in these days, they go their own way— you find this? Françoise wanted it kept secret, so . . . But, Mr Brent, I will try. It may be . . .'

'Do they have a car radio? You might ask for a message to be relayed on Françoise's favourite wavelength.'

'It's possible. I will do my best.'

'I'd be so grateful. If Peter does contact you, ask him to phone me here, will you? What car are they using?'

'A Citroën, I think. I'm not sure. It belongs to a friend of Françoise.'

'Perhaps you can find out the number and give it to the police.'

She seemed singularly ill-informed about any practical details of this excursion that had taken Peter into the mysterious byways of central France. Four teenage youngsters of both sexes, crammed together in a nameless car that was heading for nowhere in a June heatwave . . . A surge of puritanical indignation brought harsh words to

the edge of my tongue. Before they took the plunge,
however, Madame Bardeau was replying amenably.

'Give me one half-hour, Mr Brent. After that I shall
telephone you and say what I've done. Goodbye for the
moment.'

She hung up. I was left staring down at the handset,
wondering what else I should have said. The mother of
Françoise sounded capable, up to a point; but rather
more liberal-minded than I could have wished. Peter was
a reserved, studious boy, ill-suited to bohemian adven-
tures with happy-go-lucky Continental contemporaries.
Particularly when they placed him out of communication
at a time of crisis. As I dropped the receiver, Debbie
emerged from the kitchen with a tray.

'Any luck?'

'She's going to try to have Pete contacted.' I pursued
her into the living-room. 'Could take a day or more.
Apparently he and his pals have gone off into the wilds.'

'Wouldn't it be better to wait, then, till they get back?'
Gently she placed a half-full beaker on the limp palm of
her sister and held it there. 'I can't see any point in
getting him agitated. By the time he—'

'I want him to know,' I said flatly.

'You mean, you want to ask him about the photo.'

'Don't keep saying that.'

'It's true, isn't it?' By now, Carol had locked on to the
beaker and was taking desultory sips, staring listlessly
ahead. Patting her shoulder, Debbie came away and
walked over to the sliding doors. 'Right now, you can't
think of anything else.'

'Can you wonder?'

'Yes. Frankly, it does make me . . .' Staring through the
double-glazing, she stiffened abruptly. In the act of
reaching for my cup on the tray, I glanced up.

'What is it?'

'I thought I saw something. It's gone now.'

Joining her, I glared into the darkness. 'What kind of thing?'

'Not sure. A movement of some sort.' She pointed. 'Over there. Probably my imagination.'

'An owl,' I suggested. 'Or a bat.'

Debbie shook her head, then shrugged. 'Can't have been anything.'

'Perhaps I'd better take a look. You stay here.'

Collecting a flashlamp from its kitchen drawer, I let myself out into the still warmth of the night. Apart from the chittering of a grasshopper, the garden lay soundless in its shroud, cryptic as death: merely by walking across it I felt I was taking liberties. The beam of the lamp showed me familiar things in an unfamiliar pattern: conifers, rosebushes, the paving slabs that bordered the lawn. Passing through the gap in the thorn hedge at the midway point, I continued into what we grandly called the orchard, a scattering of apple and plum trees that spasmodically yielded a crop when they felt inclined and for the rest of the time did an efficient job of blocking the sunlight from the dahlias. Here, too, there was no immediate sign of disturbance. Shining the light around, I saw only turf and tree-bark. I was starting to walk back when the beam picked out something.

It lay at the foot of a Worcester apple tree, half-hidden by the longer grass about the base of the stem: a woman's shoulder-bag in glossy beige plastic-leather, on its side and with mouth agape, but its contents intact. I picked it up.

I had never seen it before. Neither Sara nor the girls, to the best of my knowledge, possessed anything of the kind. Admittedly this meant little: I was not in the habit of taking note of feminine accessories, least of all within the family. The things the bag contained were standard: lipstick, hand-mirror, comb, nail-file, purse. There was more beneath, but for the moment I stuffed it all back and then stood looking around, slowly circulating the beam, picking out the length of the close-boarded fence that encircled the orchard. Nothing unusual was in evidence.

'Anybody there?'

My call went unanswered. Having waited a few seconds, I performed a final revolution with the flashlamp before returning to the house at a casual pace. Back inside, I bolted the kitchen's outer door, stowed the flashlamp and went through to the living-room. Debbie swung around.

'Nothing?'

'Only this.' I held up the bag for inspection. She looked at it blankly. From the sofa, Carol gave it a brief survey before glancing away with an instant loss of interest. Coming forward, Debbie took it from me.

'Where did you find it?'

'Under one of the apple trees. Not yours?'

Frowning, she shook her head. 'I've never had one like this.' Releasing the hasp, she peered inside. The frown deepened.

A little breathlessly, I said, 'Could it belong to Mum?'

Another headshake, emphatic and final. 'Not her style at all. She likes the floppy sort, with zips.' She looked up. 'Under a tree? And no sign of—'

'That's all I could find. Looks new, doesn't it? Fair bit of stuff inside.'

'Perhaps there's a name and address.'

While she was emptying out the contents, the telephone rang in the hall. I ran for the door. 'That'll be Françoise's mother. She's been quick.' Leaving Debbie to examine the objects, I went outside, snatched up the receiver. 'Hullo? Madame Bardeau?'

Silence. I waited for clicks, buzzes, dial tones. Nothing happened. I rattled the instrument. 'Hallo? Can you hear me?'

My ear picked up what sounded like a sigh. Then a voice. 'Rollo? Is that you?'

It was faint, as though reaching me from another galaxy. For a moment I gaped at the wall. 'Sorry?' I said stupidly. 'Could you speak up, please.'

'Missing you, Rollo. Let me come back. It's more than . . .'

Then came the click. The dialling tone followed up, a steadfast purr. I banged the receiver rest. 'What's that? Don't ring off! Hullo!' The mechanical sound persisted remorselessly. Still I pressed the receiver to my ear. By now I had a girl at each elbow. Turning to Debbie, I rammed the receiver into her hand. 'Hear anything?'

She listened for a moment, looked at me curiously. 'Just the tone. Was it Madame Bardeau?'

'I don't know. I thought . . .' I sat heavily on the telephone stand. 'Whoever it was, she called me Rollo.'

Carol let out a squeal. Debbie clutched my arm. 'Mum! That was Mum. She's the only one who's ever called you that.'

'She *must* be all right.' Carol skipped away down the hall.

Debbie looked at me with shining eyes. 'What did she say? Is she coming home? Did she sound—'

'Hold on a minute.' My tone of voice dragged her to a halt. From the end of the hall, Carol turned to stare. I looked mutely from one to the other, stuck for a phrase. Finally I said, 'Girls, I'm sorry. It can't have been your mother.'

Debbie blinked as though I had slapped her face. 'Why not?'

'The voice. It was pretty faint, but it wasn't hers.' I put a hand to my head. 'It was a different voice entirely.'

CHAPTER SEVEN

By the time I reached the office in Wimbledon it was almost ten-thirty. As I came along the corridor I could hear Doris, the switchboard girl employed by Barrett's, the marketing firm with which I shared the first floor of the premises, asking someone if they would talk to someone: although invisible from my office door, she was far from inaudible. The chipboard partitioning saw to that. Inside my own section, the subdued clatter of Tina's electric typewriter came from her boxed-off cubicle. I went straight through to the main room, where Eleanor was in radiophone contact with Sid, our senior driver. She flipped a hand in greeting while continuing to talk.

'So how long will it take you to get back? Look, Sid, it's urgent. No, Maurice can't do it. He's stuck at Southampton, waiting for a shipment. Forget about Roxall's. They've not paid us for the last lot yet. If you go direct to Ealing . . . Yes, they're expecting you. You'll be away again inside the hour. Back home in time for the cricket. Happy? Thanks, Sid. Problem solved. See you.'

Disconnecting, she spun her revolving chair to face me. 'He's *not* happy, but I think I've chatted him round. If not, you'd better start composing a small-ad for tomorrow's paper. HGV driver wanted, must be flexible, sex no obstacle. Bit late, aren't you? What held you up?'

'Trouble at home.'

Eleanor's survey took on a new dimension. 'Somebody ill?'

'I wish I knew.'

'What's that supposed to mean?'

As I sat down, she rose and came over to place a hand lightly on my shoulder. 'Something happened?'

I explained about Sara.

'Missing?' she breathed. 'Well, well. That's what I call a turn-up.'

'It's what I call crazy.'

'I'd no idea . . .' Her fingertips slid across to my neck. 'You poor fellah. What a day you must have had.'

For a moment I experienced the familiar high-voltage kick as contact was maintained. Presently I raised my own hand, held her wrist. 'I need to talk, Linny.'

She pondered briefly before reaching a decision. Walking to the cubicle door, she opened it and glanced inside. 'Tina, Mr Brent and I will be out for half an hour. Can you look after things? There's nothing desperate. Thanks, dear. If you get a call you can't deal with, take the number and we'll get back to them.' She closed the door. The typewriter resumed its chatter. 'Come on,' she ordered, hoisting me out of the chair. 'We'll go round to Myrtle's.'

Her instinct was sound. On entry, the lively hubbub of the place started to perform its therapy on my nerve-ends. Buying coffee and biscuits at the counter, Eleanor shepherded me to a table on a raised area at the back of the shop, from which could be observed the rapacious activities of a cross-section of the local population apparently driven to frenzy by the allure of Myrtle's jam-daubed crisp doughnuts, sultana-stuffed Danish pastries and cherry-topped cheesecake. The mere fact that all this gourmet commerce was taking its normal daily course helped to calm me down. If Myrtle's customers could still make pigs of themselves at two or three pounds a time, nothing could have changed very much.

As for Eleanor . . . Waiting for the coffee to cool, I smiled at her with my eyes.

'That's my boy.' She clasped my hand under the table. 'Much better than the haunted look.'

'Not here, Linny.'

Compliantly she took her hand away. 'What are the police doing about Sara?'

'Looking for her, I suppose. After a fashion.'

'Why d'you say that?'

'They're searching for the wrong person.'

Eleanor showed her puzzlement. Swiftly I added, 'Tell me something. Would you say I was normally observant?'

She smiled wickedly. 'Depends what you're observing.'

'I'm serious. Let me try something on you.' I thought for a moment. 'He's thirty-two. Medium height and build. Slightly receding dark hair, broad forehead, snub nose, wide mouth, stained teeth . . .'

'Sid,' she said promptly.

'Full marks. What do I get?'

'Eight out of ten. You forgot about his flapping ears, but it wasn't a bad effort.' She eyed me shrewdly. 'Don't tell me, let me guess. When it came to describing Sara . . .'

'No, you're wrong. From my point of view there was no problem. I can see her face now, Linny, as plainly as I see yours.' She winced. Under cover of the table I pressed her thigh contritely. 'You know what I mean. Preference doesn't come into this. I'm talking strictly on a . . . a draughtsmanship level, if you like. Technically, the description of Sara I gave to the cops would pass any test, I'm convinced. And yet — this is the disturbing thing — it doesn't tally with the girls'.'

'If that's all you're fired up about —'

'It's not.' I explained about the photograph.

Eleanor studied me for a long time. Eventually she said, 'People can look awfully different in snapshots. I remember —'

'We've been into all that,' I said impatiently. 'This goes way beyond any question of faulty camera-angle, hazy definition — anything of that kind. I'm telling you this as a fact: the woman in that photo is not Sara.'

'Although both the girls think it is?'

'They don't think. They know. They're as positive one way as I am the other. What do you make of that?'

She pursed her lips. They were full lips, eminently pursable, but at this moment I was in no mood for facial quirks; what I sought were answers. She seemed slow in coming up with any. Presently she said, 'Has anyone else seen the print?'

I told her about the Freebodys. 'Frankly, I don't give that much for their opinion. I don't believe they'd recognize Sara if they met her in the street. But that's immaterial. The point is, they've identified the picture to the police and I can't see them changing their story now.'

'There must be others. Sisters, cousins . . .'

'The only family Sara's got are her parents, and they're both half-blind from cataracts. They live in a sheltered flat in Bromsgrove and have practically everything done for them. Showing them a photo would be like . . . describing colour to a dog.'

'Friends in the neighbourhood, then. How about her customers? She does home dressmaking, you said?'

'Yes. But she seems to have kept no record of who she's dealt with.'

'Quite a few women must have seen her, to be measured up.'

'Obviously, but if they just came to the house during the day . . .' Softly I beat the tabletop with a fist. 'There's something you've got to understand about Sara. She's always kept busy but she's never been one to mix. I've told you, haven't I? If ever I've asked her to go anywhere, she's always made some excuse. Kind of an aversion to meeting people socially. For the past few years she's barely left the house for more than an hour at a time, and when she has she's taken the car. What chance has anyone had to take notice of her?'

'Is she agoraphobic?'

'I wouldn't say so. I don't think it amounts to that.'

'If she's become a recluse . . .'

'She hasn't,' I said sharply. Eleanor looked at me. Unfurling my fist, I flapped pacific fingers. 'Well, maybe in a sense. But not an oddball. She's always been a normal, balanced person who happens to prefer a quiet existence around the house and garden. Anything wrong in that?'

'Nothing,' Eleanor said practically, 'until something like this crops up. You've told me she's on the reserved side, but I never realized . . . If only you'd shown me a picture of her some time.'

'God,' I said fervently, 'how I wish I had. Apart from not especially wanting to, I've not had one to offer. Up to yesterday, I wasn't even aware this one of Pete's existed. And now, instead of helping, all it's done is fling a spanner in the works.'

'Only where you're concerned,' she pointed out. 'Everyone else is happy with it.'

I sagged against the chairback. 'Linny, I know it sounds like paranoia, but . . . Everyone else is wrong.'

Stirring her coffee, Eleanor drank to the halfway mark. Then she brooded into the cup. During the weekend she had had something done to her hair: its coarse coppery masses had been shaped fetchingly around neck and jawline to soften the somewhat aquiline strength of her features, giving her the poise suitable for a woman of thirty-seven while skirting the matronly touch. Eleanor's supreme asset were her eyes: large, greenish and clear, with flecks of impishness. There were times when they could blaze; others when they seemed to withdraw behind translucent shutters. This was one of the latter occasions.

Uneasily I broke into the silence. 'It's the reason I'm so anxious for a word with Pete. I want to ask him about it, direct.'

Eleanor's gaze clicked into focus. 'Can't you get hold of him?'

I explained about the camping trip. 'Madame Bardeau seems to be doing her best, but the French authorities haven't traced him yet. I called her again this morning, just before I left.'

'Does she have the office number?'

'Yes. Maybe we should get back.' Suddenly restless again, I rose and walked past the pâtisserie display to the door, leaving her to catch up. Out in the sunlight, I felt a prod from the lurking headache. Coming abreast, Eleanor fell into step. I sensed that she itched to clasp my arm. 'Watch it,' I murmured. 'Eyes . . . remember.'

'Fusspot.' She stayed clear. 'What are your plans for lunch?'

'I feel I ought to stay by the phone.'

'Tina can put any calls through.' She sent me a provocative glance. 'I had my hair done specially.'

'I noticed that.'

'Well, then?'

'I don't know, Linny. One of the girls might call. Or the police.'

'If they do, I'll take the message and say I'll pass it on. Nobody can possibly know you're with me. Come on, champ. You need to relax.'

'I mustn't stay more than an hour.'

Tina's flaxen-topped head emerged from her cubicle as we re-entered the office. 'Just one call,' she announced, dividing the information impartially between us. 'They want you to ring home, Mr Brent.'

I made a dive for the phone. 'Who spoke to you?' I demanded, dialling feverishly.

The unblemished skin above Tina's nose went fleetingly into wrinkles. 'Your daughter, Deborah. At least I think it was. Sounded like her voice.'

'You should ask, Tina,' said Eleanor reprovingly. The girl flushed and withdrew.

'Debbie?' I said shakily into the mouthpiece. 'Has Mum—?'

'No, there's no news.' Her voice was duller than old paint. 'It's just that the police have been round again. Yes, Merton and somebody else. Nothing in particular. They had another look round the house. I said they could.'

'Did they stay long?'

'About twenty minutes. Oh, they took the bag with them. They want to talk to you again. I said you'd be home about five.'

'Good girl. How's Carol?'

'Pining. She's hardly eaten. I thought I'd boil a couple of eggs.'

'Try to get something into her. And yourself. 'Bye for now, sweetheart. See you before five, if possible.'

Eleanor watched me hang up. 'No developments?'

'None to shout about.' I stood staring at my desk, the wire trays, the invoices and bills of lading strewn everywhere. Nothing in sight seemed to have anything to do with me. Advancing, Eleanor took command.

'There's only one thing of any urgency—the Milthorpe query. I can deal with that. You perch yourself over there, take it easy. Try to think of anyone you've forgotten to contact. There has to be somebody.'

'Or something.' I made slowly for the window-seat. 'There's a factor missing. What it is, don't ask me, but it's been overlooked.'

Eleanor's house lay in its own secluded plot on the fringe of Wimbledon Common. Privacy was guaranteed. I followed her into the high-ceilinged hallway, dim and cool after the midday glare outside. Turning as she closed the door, Eleanor melted into my arms, performing all the required movements with practised dexterity before, choosing her moment, she breathed into my left ear.

'Back room, I think. More of a decadent atmosphere.'

She was right. The back room seemed to snigger behind its hand at sight of us. Eleanor proved to be in robust form, more than a trifle overpowering in her demands: after a while, evidently sensing my difficulty, she let up a little.

'Your mind's not on the job, Ralphie-Boo.' She threw out a bare arm to catch the sunlight on the carpet. 'What became of my little savage? Okay, okay. Let's chew it over some more.' She lay still for a moment. 'You don't think Sara somehow found out about us?'

Languidly I shook my head. 'How could she?'

'Unless some kind friend told her.'

'Who, for God's sake? We live eight miles from here. Nobody in this district has a clue who I am.'

'Anyhow, with the precautions we've taken . . . Enough for a major war.' She squinted up at me. 'Just the same, it could account for what's happened. If Sara had suddenly twigged, it might have biffed her off balance.'

'Affected her brain, you mean? She went out for a walk to think it over . . . then got hit by amnesia?'

'Or else decided to get back at you. Give you a fright, teach you a lesson.'

'And petrify the girls, too?'

'People don't always think of these things.'

For a while we were silent. Eleanor's face was turned partly away, so that all I could see was the nearer set of eyelashes, flickering erratically in response to the impulses from her brain. It was a good brain, one that I respected. Without it, she could hardly have engineered the divorce settlement she now enjoyed. Besides the house, she received a monthly allowance, index-linked. Although inadequate for her needs, it was nevertheless a comfortable footing to build on, and it came through reliably. Eleanor had taken care to maintain a good working relationship with her ex-husband, an airline pilot

with standards. When it came to working things out to
optimum advantage, Eleanor ran second to nobody.

'I take it,' she said presently, 'you've told me every little
thing there is to know?'

'About Sara?'

'About the events of yesterday.'

'There is an occurrence or two I haven't mentioned . . .'

'Oh?' She sat up, automatically steadying her hair with
a hand. In view of the total nudity of the rest of her, the
gesture had a faintly ludicrous quality: for all her
intellect—or possibly as a consequence of it—Eleanor's
mannerisms could occasionally verge upon the over-
machined. 'What is it you've avoided volunteering?'

'There's no avoidance about it. I didn't want to load
everything on you, that's all. But since you ask, we did
have a phone-call last night. Quite late. When I
answered, I heard this faint voice—male, female, young,
old, I can't be certain. It said something about missing
me and wanting to come back. Then they hung up, or
else the line was cut. I'm not sure about that, either.'

'Cheap hoax,' Eleanor said dismissively.

'I wondered.'

'You can bet on it. Some local nut who'd somehow
found out Sara was missing.'

'Yes, I'd go along with that, only . . . Whoever it was,
you see, called me by a pet name. Only she could know
about it.'

'What name is that?' Eleanor sounded a little miffed.

'Never mind. It's just one of those silly endearments. I
don't think she's used it in years. The point is, even an
acquaintance could never have heard it.'

'That strikes me as a slightly sweeping statement.
Someone else in the family could have heard her call you
by it some time, and mentioned it to someone else. You
know how these things get around.'

'Well, I admit the girls were familiar with it, but they

tend to be tight-lipped on family matters, as a rule. I
can't see them bandying it around.'

'Anything else?' Eleanor enquired, after a pause.

'The bag.'

'What bag?'

'Also last night, I found a woman's shoulder-bag in the
garden. Virtually new and unmarked.'

Eleanor blinked. 'So?'

'It wasn't there earlier in the day. The girls went all
round the garden half a dozen times, looking for Sara.
They couldn't have missed it.'

'Anything inside?'

'Nothing to give a clue to ownership. Not even a
monogrammed hankie.'

After a few moments' reflection, Eleanor heaved
herself to her feet and started to dress. Feeling foolish, a
fraud and a failure, I followed her example, and for a
while the only sound was the rustle of garments. Zipping
up her skirt, Eleanor gave her firm stomach a
congratulatory pat, peeped over a shoulder and came
across to adjust my necktie, giving the trivial operation a
sybaritism that outdid Hollywood. 'Impeccably groomed,
as always,' she murmured, slightly cross-eyed as she
concentrated. 'I think this is one of the things that get me
about you. I've never been sold on the scruff generation.
Tell me something, my dear. Do you know, or have you
ever known, anybody who lugs that kind of shoulder-bag
around with them?'

I waited before answering. 'What if I have?'

Her green eyes widened briefly. 'Whoops, pardon me. I
was just asking.' Giving the necktie a final twitch, she
turned away. 'Subject closed, yes?'

Leaving the office promptly at four, I trotted round to
the car park and, having opened the driver's door of my
Ambassador, stood back to let the baked air disperse from

the interior. As I waited, a touch on the arm made me
jump and spin.

'What are you doing here? I've told you—'

'I know. I'm sorry, Ralph.' In the mid-afternoon
intensity of the sunshine, Tina's hair looked almost
bleached; her face, in contrast, was pink and moist. She
looked taut. 'I didn't mean to hang about for you like
this, but—'

'You left at three. You've been here an hour?'

'I just had to talk. You seemed so quiet in the office. I
thought perhaps . . .' She snatched a breath. 'Nothing's
the matter, is it?'

I nodded at the car door. 'Dive in for a minute.'

Ducking inside, she scrambled across to the passenger
seat, disarranging her skirt en route. While she smoothed
herself down with a certain anxious sensuality, I got in
beside her and pulled the door nearly shut. 'My wife's
gone missing.'

'Oh.' She put a hand to her mouth. For a second or two
she assimilated the news before returning the hand to her
skirt-hem to hold it in place. 'This is why you're leaving
early,' she said, gazing at the tail of the Toyota parked in
front of us.

'I'm in a flat spin, Tina. We'll have to coast for a few
days, okay?'

'Yes, I understand. I thought it was something I'd
done. That Eleanor—'

'She's been helping me make some enquiries. Take no
notice.'

'I can't help it. She bothers me. Sometimes, when she's
looking at you . . .'

'It's just her way. Means nothing. Don't worry about
her.'

'Could you give me one little kiss, Ralph?'

I looked carefully about the car park. It was used
mainly by office workers, not shoppers: nobody else was

homebound yet. Leaning across her, I obliged sketchily, scenting the teenage eagerness and inexperience of her, stationing my palm on her upper thigh and feeling the muscle contract. When I drew back she continued to sit there, eyes and mouth partially open, hair festooning the headrest. I said softly, 'Time to go.'

She breathed out. 'Can we meet on Wednesday, same as usual?'

'We'll see. It depends how things work out.'

With her fingers on the door-catch, she hesitated. 'I hope your wife's all right,' she said stumblingly. Throwing open the door, she slid out and hurried off.

CHAPTER EIGHT

Hearing the car, Debbie came out to the driveway to meet me. 'Heard anything more?' she asked, without hope.

'Sorry, love. Nothing this end, either?' She shook her head. 'No call from France?'

'Not yet.' She pushed back her hair in a way that reminded me of Sara. 'It's Carol I'm worried about. She won't eat or do anything. I think the doctor should see her. Shall I go round? I've been trying to call the surgery, but it's engaged the whole time.'

'Maybe you'd better.' I steered her gently into the porch. 'Meanwhile I'll make some tea and sit with her. I wish I had some news to announce. That's what she really needs.'

'Dad . . .'

'Mm?'

'Why are the police so interested in looking around here? They took ages going through Mum's things. Then they searched the garden again. I told them we'd gone over every inch, but they wouldn't listen.'

A chill scuttled through me. 'It's probably because of that bag we found,' I said carelessly. 'They're hoping something else may turn up.'

Debbie looked nonplussed. 'Like what?'

'You tell me, sweetheart. I doubt if they really know what they're after. Run along, will you, and see if you can catch Dr Ellis? Tell him we think Carol needs a sedative.'

The living-room was warm but not stuffy. Debbie had partly opened a sliding door and drawn one of the curtains to block the sunlight. From her place on the sofa Carol looked up, saw my face, went back into a huddle. I sat beside her. 'Debbie's just slipped round to the doc's. She won't be long.'

'I'm not taking anything. Not till Mum gets back.'

'You can't go without sleep in the meantime.'

'Why not?'

The query floored me. Presently I said, 'I'm going to call the Bardeaus again. Pete should have been traced by now.'

'Did you have a good day at the office?'

The trite enquiry, posed in a monotone, gave me a jolt. 'So-so,' I said, rising and making for the door. 'Hard to concentrate, naturally. Eleanor told me to get away early, said she'd look after everything.'

'That was kind of her.'

Still no inflection. I stood looking back from the doorway: Carol's gaze was directed at the cushions. I said weakly, 'Well, she's like that. She's a good sort.' Carol made no further comment. I went outside to the kitchen.

In a semi-trancelike state I prepared tea and biscuits, took it all back to her, arranged the tray at her elbow. She seemed oblivious. Trying to put myself into the mind of a psychiatrist, I pulled up a nearby chair and made a show of giving great attention to the teapot spout as I poured. 'I'm having a cup of this,' I remarked, adding milk and sugar. 'Join me if you want to.'

After a while she thrust out her legs, resettled herself with some violence against the cushions. 'I don't know how you can sit there, drinking.'

'What do you suggest I do, darling?'

She looked away. 'If you'd stayed home,' she said in a muffled voice, 'you could have helped the police.'

'They knew where to find me. No sense in my neglecting the business, is there? When Mum gets back, she won't want to find us bankrupt.'

'Eleanor could look after it. You've just said so.'

'I said she was helpful. But there are certain decisions . . .' Under cover of a mouthful of tea, I thought rapidly. 'Carol, love, I understand how you feel. But don't be misled by appearances. If I sit here starving myself, is that going to help find your mother? Or if I let the business go to ruin? One just has to try to carry on. What's the alternative?'

She turned haunted eyes upon me. 'Why doesn't she phone?'

'If it's memory-loss,' I pointed out reasonably, 'she wouldn't know the number. It'll come back to her in time.'

'But why should Mum lose her memory?'

The intensity of Carol's gaze forced me to avert mine. Pretending to search the opposite wall for inspiration, I shrugged. 'There might be no single cause. Could be an accumulation of small worries — trivial problems that she hadn't talked about.' I hesitated. 'Did she ever mention anything to you?'

From her silence, I couldn't gauge whether she was considering or evading the question. What I did know, abruptly, was that I had to get out of the room. Setting down the cup, I waved at the tray. 'Help yourself, sweetheart, while I put another call through to the Continent.'

This time it was Madame Bardeau's husband who

answered. His English was less than fluent, and we had a few moments of bilingual confusion before I could ascertain that he was alone in the house, his wife was out shopping, and their daughter and her friends were still nowhere in official view although efforts the most formidable were continuing to locate them. He sounded affable but remote. Itching to ask him to get his wife to call me on her return, I felt that to do so would have implied an insulting lack of confidence in his information, and so reluctantly I rang off, after telling him that I would be in touch again later. His parting *'Au revoir'* sounded lighthearted. Not for the first time, I had the feeling that I was trying to punch a way through cottonwool. While I was still standing beside the phone, pondering my next move, the doorbell gonged.

The young man inside the porch was lean and denim-jacketed, with slightly bulging eyes. The jacket was open down the front to display a purple shirt and a buckled belt about the waist of his light yellow trousers. Resignedly I stood aside. 'If you're from the police, you'd better come in. I was expecting a colleague of yours.'

'I'm not the law, Mr Brent.' He gave me a grave, beneficent smile. 'I came to see Carol.' Observing the blankness of my face, he added helpfully, 'I'm Lionel Gooch.' He tried again. 'The curate. Carol was with me yesterday morning, helping to—'

'I do beg your pardon. It's rather a long time, I'm afraid, since I went to church.'

'No sweat.' Stepping past me into into the hall, he subjected it to a detailed examination while I closed the door. 'Sorry to hear about the wife,' he said, protruding his eyes at the telephone. 'Lousy time for you.'

'How did you come to hear about it?'

'Carol buzzed me this morning. Wanted to maul it over with someone, I guess. She—'

Ghostlike, Carol emerged from the living-room at this

moment and gave the curate a beseeching look. He advanced purposefully. 'Chin up, Carol? Punching the old Prayer Book, like I told you?'

She rested her face tearfully on his lapels. Glancing back at me, he said, 'Give us a few minutes, okay?' Steering her the way she had come, he closed the door firmly in my face.

Suddenly I felt boneless. Sitting heavily on the bottom stair, I tried my hand at some rational deliberation, wishing all the while that Debbie would return: in her absence the house seemed curiously hostile, as though silently bearing a grudge. The feeling was fanciful, of course. At present I was inclined to imagine a good deal.

What I hadn't imagined was the readiness of Carol to dissolve in tears on the receptive chest of somebody else. But then, I reminded myself, this was the young man she had a crush on. However comprehensively his personal allure might escape me, I had to accept that he was my younger daughter's current fixation and that she would turn to him as to nobody else; even her own father.

Especially, perhaps, her father. Now that I thought about it, I wasn't at all sure of the present state of our relationship. For some years I had taken her for granted, the pale-faced junior of three about the place: at some point, had she moved on while I remained clamped to the spot? Sitting there, chin in hand, I uttered a silent groan. First Debbie, now Carol. I felt like a naval cruiser under attack. If the torpedoes didn't get me, the missiles would.

The second ring of the doorbell came almost as a relief.

'This bag,' said Detective-Inspector Sinclair, holding it out for inspection. 'You're certain it couldn't belong to your wife?'

'I'm certain of nothing.' I wished he would sit down. He kept touring the kitchen, eyeing cupboard doors. 'It's not her type of thing, I gather. But who's to say she didn't buy it on impulse, as a change?'

'Who indeed?' He meditated in front of the cooker. 'But then, when would she have made the purchase? You told me she rarely goes shopping.'

'I didn't say she was housebound. She could have gone to a store, and not mentioned it. Or,' I added, cuffed by a thought, 'one of her customers could have given it to her. In part-payment for a dress, perhaps.'

Sinclair twiddled a knob on the cooker. He made no comment.

'The chief mystery,' I resumed, 'is how it got there, under the tree, some time during yesterday.'

Restoring the knob to its former position, Sinclair turned. 'Show me.'

In the garden it felt hotter than ever. Staying close to my elbow, the Inspector gave each flowerbed and shrubbery, I thought, a more than normally attentive glance as we passed. Possibly in his free time he was an amateur botanist. When I indicated the relevant tree he circled it several times, occasionally prodding a tussock of turf with the toe of his left shoe.

'I did ask your daughter, Deborah, to show me this morning,' he remarked, turning his attention to the garden boundaries. 'Only she wasn't sure exactly which tree it was. You came out here last night by yourself?'

'After Deborah thought she'd seen something.'

'Observant young lady.'

I threw him a look. 'Did she happen to mention anything else she'd noticed?'

He made no immediate reply. Walking to the nearest point of the fence, he ran his gaze along it, much as I had done with the aid of the flashlamp the previous evening, before returning with an expression that gave nothing away. 'This voice, Mr Brent, you say you heard on the phone. Did Deborah hear it too?'

'No, of course not. Before I could react, it was cut off.'

'So you're the only person who can say what it sounded like?'

'That's just what I can't say. It was nobody's voice I recognized.'

He regarded me estimatingly. 'Not enjoying a run of luck, are we? An unidentifiable photograph: an unknown handbag out of nowhere: an alien voice. Each of these—'

'Shoulder-bag,' I corrected him.

'As I say, each of these factors seems to have a common denominator. In every case, you're the sole person concerned. Noticed that?'

I stood conning the base of the tree. 'The bag,' I said restrainedly, 'is tangible enough, I'd have thought.'

'In itself. The circumstances of its discovery, on the other hand . . .'

The sentence and its unvoiced latter section hung in the breezeless air between us. 'Shall we,' he suggested, 'get back to the house? Or rather, the garage first. I'd like a quick look at your wife's car.'

Inside the stuffy double garage he gave the Ambassador's gleaming bonnet a thump with the palm of a hand on his way past to open the offside door of its dustier stablemate, the royal-blue Metro that Sara had cherished for a year. 'Patriotic family, I see,' he said, sounding neither contemptuous nor applauding. 'Anyone else bought British as well?'

'Deborah doesn't drive. If Peter needs transport, he borrows the Metro.'

'Still be able to, won't he? When he gets back.'

The remark seemed in such poor taste that I didn't bother to reply. Ducking inside the car, Sinclair established himself in the driving seat and appraised the controls. The ignition key, in accordance with Sara's practice, had been left in place. Switching on, he studied the fuel gauge. From where I stood, I could see the indicator poised at the three-quarter mark. I spoke tartly.

'We did all this yesterday. I doubt if there's much we overlooked.'

'Dicey, leaving the key available.' He clambered out. 'Even inside a lock-up garage.' He nodded across at the Ambassador. 'Get on well with that?'

'Suits me.'

'Roomy, I imagine.' He wandered round to give it closer scrutiny. 'Good and spacious. Fair load capacity, I'm told. Carry samples, do you, Mr Brent?'

'Samples? What of? I'm in road haulage.'

'I thought that's what you said. Seems a bit of a waste, then, a car this size. Just yourself using it, I mean.'

'I'm a family man, if you remember.'

'Yes. Taken the family out lately, have you?'

'There hasn't been much opportunity,' I said evenly. 'What with my wife's dressmaking and gardening, Carol's church activities, Deborah's library commitments . . .'

'Not a lot of spare time for jaunts.' Sinclair stood tapping the car's bodywork with squared-off fingertips. 'How about Peter, when he's at home? Full of his own devices, like the others? Photography, perhaps?'

I regarded the Inspector steadily. 'He's not that interested in camera work. As I explained—'

'Yes, you did explain. That's quite right.' Sinclair looked ruminatively through the side window at the passenger seat. 'He won't be going into films, then. Is he joining you in the firm?'

'All he's doing at present is coasting. Mulling alternatives. I'm—we're leaving it to him to decide.'

'Very sensible. Anyhow, as I was saying, you don't seem to have much use for the spare capacity in this, just now. Except, I suppose, when it comes to friends, colleagues . . .'

Stooping abruptly, he opened the Ambassador's near-side door, leaned inside, groped with a hand. Emerging, he held something under my chin. 'Looks like one of your passengers was unlucky. Left their mascot behind.'

On the centre of his fleshy palm lay the silver crucifix
and chain that Tina never failed to wear about the neck.
I gave it a suitably startled look. 'Good Lord. I can guess
how that happened. It belongs to my office typist, and
she —'

'The lady ought to do something about that clasp.' He
displayed it solemnly. 'If it's apt to come adrift when she's
just sitting in the front seat of a car . . .'

'I had to pull up sharply and she got jerked forward.
That's when it must have happened.'

'No seat-belt?'

'She was only going half a mile. She wanted the shops,
so I dropped her off. She'll be glad to have this back.'

'Tell her the first half-mile can be as dangerous as all
the rest.' He allowed me to take the crucifix. 'Quite apart
from which,' he added severely, 'it also happens to be the
law. Not anxious to spoil her looks too soon, is she? Is she
a looker?'

'Attractive, you mean? Reasonably. In the modern
style.'

'Much the same age-group as your daughters, I dare
say?' He closed the car door. The thud echoed from the
garage roof.

'A little older.' Involuntarily, my toes performed
squirming motions of their own inside my shoes.

With a final, lingering look around, Sinclair strolled
out of the garage to stand by the kitchen door, once more
contemplating the garden. Stowing the crucifix in a
pocket, I joined him and waited. Without shifting his
gaze, he said musingly, 'You're a conscientious man, Mr
Brent, if I may say so.'

'How do you mean?'

'With all the worry, I'd have thought you might have
given work a miss today. But then, maybe you wanted
something to occupy your mind.'

★

Debbie was beating up eggs in a basin. She said, 'The doctor has a lot of people to see, but he might call about eight.'

Sinclair looked interested. 'Doctor?'

'For Carol,' I explained.

'Taking it hard, is she?' Lowering himself uninvited on to the nearest stool, he took an envelope from his breast pocket, placed it on the worktop, lifted the flap. 'I've brought that photo back. We've had copies made, but before doing anything with them I wanted to give you the chance to . . .'

'Good.' With some eagerness I advanced. I was avid for another look at it. Sliding the print out of the envelope, Sinclair positioned it where we could both see.

Debbie spoke first. 'The answer's still the same.'

He cocked an eye at me. After a few more seconds I said slowly, 'I'm sorry, but quite honestly . . .'

'To you, it's still a lousy picture?'

'Have I ever said that? As far as one can tell, there's nothing wrong with the photograph. The thing that's wrong—'

'I know, I know. It's not your wife.' He turned back to Debbie. 'Any further comment on that?'

'Only that I don't understand.' Her voice was tight. 'I've identified it as my mother. So has my sister. And the neighbours. What more do you want?'

'We'd prefer it to be unanimous,' he said mildly, 'within the family. We'd hate to circulate the wrong picture and hound down some total stranger sheltering in Bournemouth.'

'It's not the wrong picture!'

Sinclair's wry glance returned to me. 'Ball's back in your court, I'm afraid. How about it, Mr. Brent? Do we go ahead and put this picture out? Or do we wait for final confirmation from this son of yours who took it?'

'I'd feel easier.' I looked appealingly at Debbie.

'Forgive me, darling, but when there's such a clash of opinion . . . Don't you think Pete should arbitrate?'

She delivered the shrug that seemed to have become the staple feature of her responses. 'It's up to you.' Turning away, she transferred the mangled eggs into a saucepan which she dumped on a ring of the cooker. Sinclair eyed her rigid back for a moment before getting up with a puff.

'Is Carol in any state to be questioned?'

'There's someone with her. The curate from St Luke's.'

'Oh yes?' Sinclair grabbed the photograph. 'We could try this on him.'

I said, 'I doubt whether—'

Already he was striding out of the kitchen. With an unhappy glance at Debbie, absorbed in her cookery, I tailed him to the living-room where the Rev. Lionel Gooch was in earnest, *sotto voce* conversation with a pallid but noticeably more animated Carol, seated next to him on the sofa and clutching his hand. Sidestepping the prong of sheer jealousy that was thrusting for my vitals, I cut in ahead of the Inspector and made the introductions. The curate's protuberant orbs subjected Sinclair to a visual blitz. 'Carol's in shock,' he said severely. 'Go easy on her, okay?'

Lifting his brows at me, Sinclair proffered the photograph. 'Take a look at this, Mr Gooch. Can you tell us who it is?'

The curate gazed at it blankly. 'I'm afraid not.'

Sinclair's raised brows hurtled together. 'You don't recognize her?'

'It's Mrs Brent, I assume? I've never met the lady. She's not an active church member and she doesn't—'

'Right. Thanks.' The Inspector's glance switched to Carol. 'No change in your view? You still maintain it's your mother?'

She nodded. Gooch looked around in mystification. 'Is

there some doubt about it?'

'Only in my case,' I informed him. 'I don't consider it's an acceptable likeness. Did — does my wife know anyone else at the church?'

'Search me,' he said cheerfully. 'I'll make enquiries, if you like. Have you asked the Vicar?'

Carol spoke up suddenly. 'Mum never had anything to do with the church. You know that, Dad.'

'Maybe I should, but then I'm not here during the day.' What I intended as a cool disclaimer emerged more as a whine. 'I thought it was just possible she might have attended coffee mornings, that kind of thing . . .'

'She never has.' Carol's voice was decisive, stronger. 'She's always been far too busy.'

Removing the photograph deftly from the curate's hand, Sinclair restored it to the envelope before backing to the door.

'I'll be on my way, then. You'll let us know, Mr Brent, the moment you get word from your son? The more accreditation we can get of this snapshot, the better for all concerned. Goes without saying.' He flapped me away. 'Don't bother, I'll find my own way out. And don't lose heart, any of you. We'll keep looking, believe me. We don't give up that easily.'

CHAPTER NINE

'You sound anti-fuzz,' said Eleanor. 'Any reason?'

'It's just their attitude. I've no specific cause for complaint, except that merely because I'm saying one thing and everyone else is saying another . . .' Taking a breath, I lowered my voice. 'I suppose one can't blame them, altogether. Like me, they're confused. But I still don't care for Sinclair's manner. Forget that for now.

Anything happening your end that I should know about?'

'Sid managed the Ealing job. Now he's flogging across to South Wales with the load for Willerby's. Maurice is on his way back from Oxford, or should be. He's due for a rest, so the Ipswich trip will have to wait. Aside from that, there's just the new contract to be cleaned up and finalized — I can be sorting that out with Cliff. He's been through it with you, hasn't he, plugging the loopholes? So there's no need for you to come over unless you start going bananas at home.'

'I do feel I should stick around. It's not fair on the girls to leave them, and I'm hoping Peter might call. I'd better hang up now, leave the line clear. Oh, Eleanor . . .'

'Uh-huh?'

'Could you give Tina a message? Ask her to take the correspondence she was doing for me round to the Post Office this afternoon, register it and send it off. Will you do that?'

'Sure. Anything else?'

'Just wish me luck. I feel in need of some.'

'You can have all the luck in the world, if you still love me.'

'Of course. See you soon. 'Bye for now.' I dropped the receiver as Debbie came into the hall. 'Breakfast ready, sweetheart?'

'If you feel like swallowing.'

'I don't, but we have to. Carol staying in bed?'

'She still seems dopey. Compared with those useless pills, that stuff of the doctor's must be lethal. I'll try her later with something to eat.' Debbie regarded me in silence for a moment. 'Are you going to the office?'

'No. Eleanor can cope.'

We sat down to grilled bacon at the kitchen table. Although the weather had changed a little for the cooler and cloudier, Debbie still wore a short-sleeved blouse and summerweight skirt; there was something Sara-like about

her, Sara as she had been when we married, daisy-fresh,
with stocks of strength and resource tucked quietly away.
I caught myself speculating, not for the first time, on life
at the Public Library. There must be more to it, I
guessed, than the endless restoration of volumes to
shelves, the feminine backchat that my imagination had
originally conjured up. Male staff, for instance. Assessing
her across the table, I wondered how much havoc she had
created already. Through a mouthful of toast I said,
'How about you? Will they be needing you back?'

'I've explained to Mrs Bagshott. She told me to stay
away as long as necessary.'

'You don't have to, you know. If you'd sooner—'

She gave a jerk of the head. 'I couldn't concentrate.
Besides, there's Carol to look after.'

'I can do that.'

'There ought to be two of us here. I'll need to go
shopping, and you may get an urgent call from the office
at any time.'

'As a matter of fact—' I gave close attention to the
buttering of a fresh slice— 'I'll have to run over there this
afternoon. Just for a short while.'

'Something Eleanor can't handle?' The question was
put without intonation, and yet for some reason it stung
my face.

'I have to sign some cheques, give the go-ahead on a
contract.' I glanced up. 'Commercial life goes on.'

She nodded in a neutral way. 'In case Mum comes
back.'

After a silence I said, 'You talk as if you don't expect
her to.'

'Do you?'

I hunted for words. 'Yes, of course. If anything had
happened to her, we'd have heard by now. It has to be
amnesia. It'll wear off, I'm telling you.' I forced the

sketch of a grin. 'Your mother's too domesticated to stop away for long.'

Again the dispassionate nod. 'Did you mind her being like that, Dad?'

'Domesticated? I never really . . . You can't change the way a person's made.'

'But sometimes you can adapt to it.'

'Meaning I didn't?'

She rose and took her plate to the sink. Her manner filled me with disquiet. With increasing frequency, I was getting the message that Debbie saw a great many things a lot more clearly than I had assumed; beyond this, her reactions were an enigma. I felt cut off. Joining her at the sink, I was careful to maintain a physical gap of an inch or two between us, much as I longed to re-establish contact. 'I do wish,' I remarked, keeping it casual, 'Pete would hurry up and phone.'

'If he does, it won't change anything.' She moved away to collect a tea-towel.

'How's that?'

'He'll just say the photo is the one he took at Christmas. What else can he say?'

'I wasn't only thinking of that. But in any case, I'm not arguing. Remember? We agreed last night that the cops should be authorized to use the picture if they want.'

'But you're still not convinced.'

For a few moments I rinsed dishes in silence. Drying and polishing them scrupulously, Debbie carried them to various parts of the kitchen and hid them away, rather as if she were cataloguing books at the library: her application to most tasks was beyond criticism. A shade of imperfection here and there would almost have been welcome, I thought treacherously. It was a senseless quibble. Without her, I should have been lost. Her down-to-earth housewifery was keeping things ticking over, and I knew we owed her a debt.

'The main reason I'd like Pete to ring,' I said presently, 'is to ask whether he used any trick lighting when he took the snap. Or anything of that sort which might . . . have a bearing on the way I'm seeing it. Purely for my own satisfaction.'

Debbie said nothing. We finished the washing-up in a brittle taciturnity from which I was glad to escape to the garage: I wanted to check the Ambassador's oil-level, and while I was out there I put in hand another intensive search of the Metro, without significant result. After that I roamed the garden. Nothing else of an inexplicable nature had appeared during the night. Everything looked normal.

If the weather had remained hot, the park would have been alive. But it was twenty degrees cooler and drizzling, and one of the only two people in sight was an elderly keeper who was pecking at a shrubbery border with a hoe.

The other, in vivid green mackintosh and rain-hat, was waiting at the usual spot, next to the giant oak by the entrance to a hedge-enclosed alcove under the shelter of a high wall topped with broken glass sunk into mortar. Seizing my arm, Tina impelled me into concealment. 'Eleanor gave me your message about the Post Office.' She turned with shining eyes. 'I guessed what it must mean.'

She tilted her face. I gave her parted lips a brief kiss, then renewed the salutation as she seemed to expect more. She sighed, relaxed against me. 'Heavenly. Seems an age since last time.'

'Only yesterday,' I protested.

'That didn't count.' Keeping hold of me, she stood off with a light frown of observation. 'Any news of your wife?'

'None, I'm afraid. That's what I wanted to talk to you about.'

Apprehension stole into her demeanour. 'What?'

'Only that I've got to watch my step for a while.'

'Why?'

'I don't want to give the police any cause for suspicion.'

Her alarm and perplexity deepened. 'I don't see what you're getting at.'

Easing her towards the bench seat at the rear of the enclosure, I pushed her gently down and sat facing her. The varnished wood was damp, but we were both well protected. 'Men whose wives have gone missing,' I explained, 'tend to come under scrutiny. If the police found that you and I were involved, they might start thinking nasty thoughts. And you could be implicated. We don't want that, do we?'

She moved with a trace of impatience. 'Does it matter what they think?'

'Yes,' I said firmly. 'It does. Suspicion and conjecture can lead to all sorts of unpleasantness. Best to let this blow over, then pick up the threads again.'

She pouted. 'That could be days — weeks. Why can't we just carry on? Nobody can possibly know we're meeting.' She brightened. 'Come to that, why not use this to bring things to a head? You've always said it was just a matter of the right situation arising, so that you could make the break. This is it, surely?'

I nodded slowly, thinking fast. 'Something in that. On balance, though, I'd sooner give it a few days at least. See how things pan out.' Tenderly I chucked her chin. 'You can wait a bit longer, can't you?'

Nibbling at my fingertips, she shook her head. 'Not sure. I get so lonesome. You know how I feel about you, Ralph. Sometimes in the office, I feel as if I'm going mad when that Eleanor looks at you in the way she has. I could swear she's in love with you herself.'

'Don't be silly.'

'It's not silliness,' she insisted. 'You wouldn't notice anything — men never do. But I can tell by her behaviour.

Little things, here and there. They all add up.'

'You're just jealous.'

'Do you blame me?' She sank her head against my shoulder. 'I've already got your wife to contend with. If Eleanor started to muscle in, I'd really be at my wits' end. I don't think I could take it.'

'There's nothing to "take".' My mind was racing in circles. 'You're simply imagining things. It'll all smooth out, you'll see.'

'You won't ever leave me?'

'Of course not.'

'How long before we can get married?'

'If it's a schedule you're after,' I said chidingly, 'you've picked on a bad time, Tina my precious. I've just this minute explained—'

'Yes, I know. I'm sorry.'

Her face came up and her lips parted again. Her skin was rain-flecked. The mackintosh crackled under my touch as she moved urgently against me. Desperately I tried to bring to mind our last intimate encounter, to recapture my feelings on that occasion: it was futile. There wasn't a spark I could whisk into life. Convinced that she must detect the limpness of my response, I was staggered when, taking a breather, she murmured into my chest, 'There'll never be anyone like you, Ralph. I know it. You make me feel so . . . womanly.' On a note of faint anguish she added, 'I just hope I'm good enough for you.'

I said lightly, 'I seem to have put up with you so far.'

'You wouldn't prefer me with dark hair? I could, you know. I've several wigs at home.'

'If I'd wanted a brunette I'd have gone after one.'

'Darling.' She renewed the assault. Again my reply lacked sparkle, but it seemed to satisfy her. She peeped up at me, her lashes fluttering. 'Have you got the car?'

'Yes, but—'

'Let's take it up on to the Common.'

'I can't, Tina. Not now.'

'We needn't be long. It's all right in the back seat.'

'Someone might see us.'

'Not if we go to the usual place.' She sat up, studying me more closely. 'You've not been so cautious before. What's the problem?'

'The problem is, love, I've got to get home. My wife's missing and my daughters are waiting for me. I'm not a free agent, right now.' Disengaging myself, I stroked wet hair away from her eyes, which blinked under my touch. Her facial skin, though moist, gave out heat that I could feel. She sighed, and sagged.

'All right. I suppose I'd better let you go. When can we—?'

'The moment things quieten down. That's a promise. Now I must be off. Did you tell Eleanor you'd go back to the office?'

'No,' she said dully. 'She said I might as well go on home.'

'Sound advice.' Giving her a final kiss, I stood up and hauled her with me. 'You dropped this inside the car yesterday,' I told her, pressing the silver crucifix into her palm. 'Better have the clasp looked at.'

'Oh! I wondered where it had got to.' She tucked it carefully into her bag, a jet-black, glossy affair with a shoulder-strap, not unlike the one I had found in the garden. Snapping it shut, she looked up at me soulfully. 'It's not sinful, Ralph, what we're doing, is it? Not when we love each other so much?'

I shook my head. 'The only sin,' I said reassuringly, 'is when you cause harm to other people.'

Eleanor was dictating a letter into the audio. Switching off at my arrival, she sat up. 'Holy Jerusalem. I wasn't expecting you this time of day. Something happened?'

'Nothing positive.' I fell exhausted into my chair. 'Just thought I'd get out of the house for an hour. I can't stay. Any hitches?'

'All flowing smoothly.' She was observing me with attention. 'Cliff's gone back to draw up the revised contract, and I was about to leave myself. Tina went earlier. You look played out. So . . . nothing fresh on the home front?'

'Only as regards the photograph.' Her eyebrows put the question. 'I've told the cops,' I explained, 'to circulate it if they see fit.'

'Aha. You've decided the girls are right?'

'I still think they're as wrong as hell.'

'But in that case—'

'I can't fight it, Linny. Not any more. They'll have me locked up. Something, somewhere is wrong, but I can't place a finger on the spot and in the meantime I'm liable to be accused of not wanting Sara to be found: which isn't true.'

'But if the photo—'

'To my eyes, that snap is of someone else. Does it really matter, though? This is what I've been asking myself, and I've decided it doesn't. If it's another woman and the cops track her down, there's no special harm done. So I thought, to hell with it. Let 'em send it round, see what transpires.'

Eleanor nodded abstractedly. 'Is that what they're going to do?'

'Search me. This guy Sinclair who's handling the enquiry, he doesn't give much away. He might think it's a bit soon.'

'He could be right. Only the third day, isn't it?'

'Seems like a month.'

'Any word from Peter?'

'Nope.' Picking up a file from the desk, I glanced through it vacantly and put it down. 'I rang through again before I came out. Still no trace.'

Eleanor frowned at her nails. 'That's a little weird. First Sara, now him. You're quite sure she hasn't —'

'There can't be a connection. He's gone off with friends, that's all, and they've lost themselves in rural France. They'll show up again soon.'

'This is what the Frenchies are telling you.'

'What do you mean by that?'

'My dear, I haven't a clue. It just seems rather extraordinary to me that two members of your family, in effect, have gone missing at the same time. Don't you think?'

Shaken, I sat thinking hard. In a handful of words she had crystallized all the dim misgivings I had been nursing for the past forty-eight hours, assembled them into a single oracular lump, set it before me for analysis. Up to now, I had succeeded in persuading myself subconsciously that what Madame Bardeau and her genial husband kept telling me was entirely reasonable in the circumstances: their daughter and her friends had taken Peter off for a few days and, temporarily, couldn't be contacted. At this point, I had to face facts. Was it likely, or even feasible, that responsible parents would calmly permit such an escapade involving a youthful guest from another country? Whichever way I examined the thesis, it fell apart. Still partly in trance, I became aware of Eleanor's bright eyes upon me: I gained the impression she had been tracking my thoughts. I flipped a restless hand.

'You're right. I don't like it.'

'Isn't there something you can do?'

'Like, contact the French police myself?'

'I don't see why not. This Inspector Sinclair character — can't he help?'

'I'll put it to him,' I said, with sudden decision.

'I think you might be well advised.' Her pupils became

semi-opaque. 'Like to come back to the house for a while?'

'No, Linny. Thanks all the same. I told Debbie I'd just be an hour.'

'Suit yourself.' Eleanor continued to study me. 'What you said just now — about it not being true that you don't want Sara found. You mean that?'

I gaped at her. 'For God's sake. What a thing to say.'

Her slender, manicured fingers alighted upon the massive glass paperweight that stood on a corner of her desk, slid idly over its rounded surface. 'I didn't think you felt much for her, that's all.'

'Things are never that uncomplicated.' I groped for a way of putting it. 'After so many years, you get sort of . . . attuned to a person. There's a bond. To be honest, Linny, I'm not absolutely clear about my feelings for Sara. In a way, I feel protective towards her. Responsible. Know what I mean?'

Eleanor said nothing, which took me aback. I had expected a reply of instant comprehension. To mask the silence, I went stumbling on. 'Apart from all that, there are the children. Debbie and Carol are both prostrate with shock and anxiety. How could I hope that Sara won't come back to them?'

'They'd get over it.' She spoke without emotion. 'And as far as you're concerned, Sara's permanent disappearance would be an almighty bonus, I'd have thought.'

For a moment I was dumbstruck. 'What in the world are you talking about?'

'Ralphie my pet, get a grip on yourself. No wife equals no maintenance demands, equals freedom and bliss. Do I have to spell it out?'

My recovery was gradual. I said slowly, 'You're talking as if I'd been planning all along to divorce Sara and re-marry.'

'Shouldn't I be?'

I jumped up. 'The idea's nonsensical,' I said angrily. 'Even if I'd wanted to, I couldn't now. Not without a presumption of death or something, and it's a trifle early to be—'

'Okay, forget about re-marriage. Take another hypothetical situation—setting up home with someone else, for example. Sara's absence would solve any amount of problems there, you have to admit.' Eleanor gave a sudden chuckle. 'Actually, it might be the quickest way to fetch her back. If that's what you really want.'

'Who else,' I demanded incautiously, 'would I be hankering to set up home with?'

'That,' she said coolly, 'is for you to say. One thing I'll tell you, though, for nothing. I know who'd be entitled to first refusal.'

In the stillness that ensued, I became conscious of the jerking second-hand of the electric clock. It was trying to tell me something. Five-fifteen: that was the message. Debbie would have been expecting me back, twenty minutes ago.

Finally I muttered something. Eleanor leaned forward, curved a hand about an ear. 'You didn't realize I felt that way? Funny thing about men. For reasonably intelligent creatures, they can be incredibly obtuse at times.' Coming to her feet, Eleanor placed a hand on each of my shoulders and looked me in the eyes. Behind her smile, steel thread ran through the velvet. 'Being of the male gender—and there's certainly no dispute about that, I'm happy to say—you saw things going on comfortably like this for ever. Twice a week with good old Eleanor, work permitting: then home to the little wife and loving brood. Isn't that it? You overlooked the possibility that I might have an idea or two of my own.'

'That's not true, Linny.'

'Prove it, then. Make an honest woman of me.'

'You know I can't. Not as things—'

She laughed amusedly, displaying a couple of gold-capped molars. 'Don't palpitate, my pet. I'm not that frantic. All I want is an understanding . . . kind of a covenant for the future. That's not asking for so much, is it?'

'It's asking more than you realize.'

'Well, thanks a lot. I'm flattered.' She spoke good-humouredly, with a self-assurance that sent my stomach crashing. 'No girl could seek a more wholehearted commitment. Luckily, I don't have to rely on your personal feelings in the matter.'

'Just what are you insinuating by that?'

Her right hand deserted my shoulder, dealt my cheek a series of playful taps. 'Work it out,' she said teasingly.

CHAPTER TEN

All the way home in the car, I worked it out.

Not the implied threat itself. That needed no dissection. Eleanor knew, and knew I was aware she knew, all that was necessary of my potentially ruinous tax and VAT manipulations, details of which I had insanely bragged about during our intimate moments. What called for cool appraisal—of the type I was at present in poor shape to give—were, first, the likely consequences of any revelations on her part; and secondly, her readiness to make them.

Suddenly her business competence and involvement with the firm's affairs, which I had valued, presented themselves as an unspeakable menace. They gave her a lever which she would not hesitate to use. After the fifth mile, no doubt of this remained in my mind. Ruthlessness and Eleanor went together like ham and eggs.

One question remained. What exactly was she after?

An undivided claim upon my affections? The notion had its flattering side, but common sense told me that more was at stake. Physically compatible though we were, Eleanor was hardly the type to lose her head like a schoolgirl on that basis alone: there had to be something more. A share in the firm. Even, possibly, a controlling interest. Possession of both man and money-machine. To a woman like Eleanor, what prospect could be more enticing?

I wondered what had held her back until now.

That didn't take long to work out, either. While Sara was around, Eleanor had been resigned to biding her time, unwilling to antagonize me by tightening the screws. Now, in her estimation, the moment had arrived. I was shaken, I was vulnerable, and there seemed a strong likelihood that Sara had obligingly removed herself from the scene. The time had come to strike, and strike Eleanor had, like a cobra. Now, all she had to do was stand back, observe the effects of the venom.

For a mile or two I toyed with the concept of buying her off. A hike in salary: a lump-sum payment: a partnership. The futility of such half-measures came at me again and again, like a fly at a window. When Eleanor played, she played to win. She had told me as much, on several occasions, and I believed her. Myself and all that I owned: this was now her objective. She wouldn't be fobbed off with less.

Meanwhile, there was Tina.

The electric fire in the living-room was switched on, and the girls were sitting side by side on the sofa in overpowering heat. Carol had got dressed. They looked as if they had stopped conversing just as I entered the room. I threw them an unconvincing smile.

'Had a few things to sort out at the office,' I explained, stationing myself near the fire in a bid to convey approval of its use. 'Then the traffic was thicker than I expected on the way home. No news?'

Debbie shook her head. I looked at Carol. 'Get some sleep?'

'Awful dreams. Now I've got a headache.'

'Inevitable. Like some tea?'

'Inspector Sinclair wants to see you again,' said Debbie.

'What time will he be here?'

'He'd like you to call in at the station.'

'Now?'

'Soon as possible, he said.'

They sat looking up at me, the pair of them, their faces blank. I glanced at the clock. 'Ten to six. Might as well get it over. I've a few questions to ask him, as well.' At the door, I looked back uncertainly. Neither of them had stirred. 'If you want a meal or anything,' I said stupidly, 'don't wait.'

In the course of the drive to the police station, I discovered that my brain had ceased to function. The imprint of the two girls, motionless on the sofa, gazing at me, was etched into its memory bank: no other information intruded. In some respects the condition was a relief, although the ability to continue reasoning and anticipating would have had its advantages.

Sinclair was again at his desk, but this time he wasn't alone. At a small table by the window sat Detective-Constable Merton, notepad and ballpoint in front of him. In deference to the weather-change, he had covered his shirt — pale orange, this one — with a suede jacket, un-zipped, carrying a spare ballpoint in its breast pocket. He looked at me without a hint of recognition. Sinclair waved me into my original chair.

'Thanks for coming, Mr. Brent. A few questions.' Merton's presence he ignored. From the corner of an eye, I saw the ballpoint picked up from the table. 'Get things sorted out at your place of work?'

'Thank you, yes.'

'Awkard for the self-employed,' he said reflectively. 'Only themselves to look after their interests. Unless, of course, they're lucky enough to have helpful staff. Which I take it you have?'

'They're soldiering on without me.'

'That's something, at any rate.' He shuffled some papers on his desk, humming unmelodiously, snatching breaths in mid-phrase. Keeping his gaze down, he added, 'You must have the knack of keeping 'em happy. Work hard at that, do you, Mr Brent?'

'I thought we were here to talk about my wife.'

'That's what we're doing,' he said on a note of faint surprise. 'Your wife and associated matters. Now let's see. Far as the admin's concerned, you've a couple of secretarial treasures at the office, I believe. A personal assistant, Mrs Eleanor Somerville, plus one typist, Miss Christina Harwood—that right?'

'Quite correct,' I said, as he paused. 'What does this have to do with my wife's disappearance?'

He made a speculative gesture. 'Just what a few others would like to know.'

I looked at him, I hoped, steadily, although there was a pitching sensation inside my head as though someone had released a large ball-bearing that was rolling from place to place, disturbing the balance. 'I don't think I understand what you're driving at.'

A small sound came from the window. It could have been a sigh.

Apparently unconscious of it, Sinclair regarded me with an air of sadness. 'As an investigative force, Mr Brent, we're not blind, deaf or dumb, you know. We do ask questions. We do get around.'

'That's comforting. I was meaning to—'

'In your case, as it happens, we've not stopped at asking questions.'

I kept command of my limbs, which were showing an inclination to twitch. 'What do I infer from that?'

'Anything you like,' he said cheerily. 'Fond of exercise, are you, sir?'

'Why do you ask?'

'I was wondering if you enjoyed your stroll this afternoon. Nice selection of parks and open spaces in the Wimbledon area, I'm sure you'd agree. Too inviting to miss, even on a rainy day.'

I said tightly, 'You had me followed.'

Leaning back, he slanted his head towards the window. 'DC Merton can answer that for you. Alec?'

Flipping the leaves of his notepad, Merton found the page he wanted, settled himself, began to read in a monotone. 'Four-eleven p.m., subject drove into car park off High Street, left car, walked briskly to nearby park entrance, took left-hand path to far corner. Entered hedged enclosure. Was there met by—'

'All *right*!' I struck the desk with a fist, rattling the Inspector's stationery equipment. 'So I met someone. What concern is it of yours? How dare you tail me around! How long has this been going on?'

'We don't need,' Sinclair said imperturbably, 'to account to you for our actions, Mr Brent. But since you feel strongly on the issue . . . It's been in progress for a couple of days. And the reason? Well, I mean to say, look at it from our standpoint. Here's a man who tells us he's lost his wife, but can't identify a picture of her . . . don't you feel we might have been open to criticism if we hadn't pursued that small matter? It started out, I can assure you, as pure routine. And got progressively more intriguing as it went along.'

'Glad to have provided entertainment.' My heart was hurling itself repeatedly against my rib-cage.

'Don't get the wrong idea. With a local crime wave on our hands—burglaries, muggings, you name it—we don't waste manpower on this sort of thing for our own amusement. Or anyone else's. If it seems justified . . .' Sinclair broke off to give his junior another significant glance. More sheets reversed themselves under Merton's questing thumb.

'Monday, twelve-fifteen,' he read. 'Subject and female left Wimbledon office building, drove in female's car to house near Common, entered together. Stayed forty minutes. On emergence, couple were clasping hands with evident strong degree of affection, exchanged protracted kiss in shelter of porch before returning to—'

'I don't have to listen to this.'

'We don't have to make it available to you,' Sinclair countered. 'I just thought it might be a helpful idea. Cards face-up on the table.'

Aware that I was sitting in a hunched position, I straightened up self-consciously. An assortment of evasions scampered through my brain, to be summarily dismissed. Nothing I said would help.

'You've been thorough.'

Sinclair acknowledged the tribute with a further grave tilt of the head.

'But,' I added, 'you'd be sensible not to read more into it than is there. All right. I do have relationships of a sort with Mrs Somerville and my typist. But let me emphasize this. It's all highly discreet and it has nothing whatever to do with the mystery concerning my wife. That I can swear.'

Sinclair sat looking into space. 'Does Mrs Somerville,' he enquired presently, 'know of your, um, attachment to Miss Harwood? Or vice versa?'

'Certainly not.'

'What makes you so sure?'

'Because each of us has always taken the utmost care.'

'How long is "always"?'

'Three or four years, in the case of Mrs Somerville. A

few months, Miss Harwood.'

'And in all this time, working in the same office, you've kept the two relationships entirely self-contained? Not a hint, not a whisper?'

'With a certain amount of diplomacy, it's simple enough.'

'Besides which, you've managed to keep both liaisons from your wife?'

'Absolutely.'

He pondered before glancing up once more. 'Something of a strain, I imagine.'

'I think that's my business.'

'In normal circumstances, Mr Brent, I'd be the first to agree. As things stand, it's been made part of our business, whether we like it or not. Your wife's missing, you see, and it's our job to try and find her.' He displayed a sudden double row of front teeth across the desk. 'On the face of it, sir, she'd every reason to take herself off.'

'She might have had. If she'd known.'

'You still maintain she didn't?'

'Not unless someone had told her in the past few days.'

'She'd given no sign of that?'

I thought deeply. 'If she did,' I said finally, 'I missed it.'

'Would you say you were alert to your wife's moods?'

'As much as most husbands.'

He made a grunting noise in his throat.

'Anyway,' I said, 'she sounded quite normal on Sunday, when she called out from the hall . . .'

'Well, she would, wouldn't she?'

'What do you mean?'

'If she were planning to skip, she wouldn't want to arouse your suspicions.'

'This idea of her "skipping",' I said wrathfully, 'is totally absurd. Even if she was upset, she wouldn't knowingly have taken such a course. I'm certain of it. And besides, nothing supports that explanation. She took

nothing with her. Clothes, money, personal belongings—
all left behind. Not to mention her car.'

'I'm glad you raised those points,' Sinclair murmured.

Leaning forward again, he started to doodle on the
margin of a typed sheet in front of him. 'They've been
exercising our minds, too. Mark you, it's not uncommon
in cases of amnesia. But you've rather done your best to
scotch the loss-of-memory supposition: you can't see any
reason why your wife should suddenly have fallen victim
to that. Yes?'

'I keep saying so.'

'Which leaves two other main possibilities. One is, she's
been kidnapped. But you've heard nothing—aside from a
cryptic phone-call which seemed to be meaningless—and
in any case you're not, if you'll forgive me, the moneybags
of South-West London. Hardly the obvious victim of a
ransom demand. Fair assessment? The other . . .'

He came to a pause.

'The other alternative,' I supplied helpfully, 'is that she
went off on purpose.'

'And here, we come back to the fact that she left
empty-handed. Is that logical? At the very least, you'd
think she'd have taken a spot of cash.'

'She may have had some in a purse.'

'Not a lot, though. According to what you and your
elder daughter have told us, she disliked having loose
money around. Most of her earnings from dressmaking,
she seems to have given to you or Deborah to bank for
her. And your monthly housekeeping cheque went
straight on to her account. Unless she had some other
source of income, she couldn't have had much to hand.'

'Her bank statement—'

'I was coming to that. The latest one in her personal
file, dated a week ago, shows a sizeable balance: obviously
she hadn't been drawing on it. And the same applies right
up to the weekend. Her current cheque-book is still there

in the file, practically unused. The only cheque she's drawn in the past two weeks was for the telephone bill.' Sinclair peered at me. 'Has she always dealt with the household accounts?'

'Yes. Out of her allowance.'

'So, what we're up against here is a situation where everything that might have been essential — cheque-book, driving licence, spare clothing, keys — was left in her bedroom; and the probability of her having any significant amount of cash with her is fairly remote. You go along with that?'

'I suppose I have to.'

He glanced towards the window, which was beginning to be lashed by a downpour. Uncoiling to his feet, Merton slammed the upper sash the ultimate two inches into place, cutting out the raindrops that were spattering his table. Stretching over the desk, Sinclair switched on an adjustable lamp and aimed the beam at a point impartially between us. 'Summer,' he observed, 'seems to have done a vanishing act, too. Cup of tea or coffee, Mr Brent?'

'I'd prefer to get along, if you don't mind. I'm anxious to be with my daughters.'

'Understandable. I'm afraid, though, they'll have to wait a bit.'

An exasperated sound escaped me. 'What else is there left to discuss?'

Without answering, Sinclair left his chair and strolled to the window, looking out at the torrent. Merton sat poker-faced, finishing off a note. The desk-lamp cast shadows. I spoke to the Inspector's back.

'Has this interview been recorded?'

'It's being recorded.'

'How much more is there likely to be?'

Turning, he lumbered back to his seat, made another finicky adjustment to the lamp's focal point. Only an outline of his face was visible to me. 'That rather depends.'

'On what?'

'Progress.' The chair creaked as he redistributed his bulk. 'I want to ask you about your wife's medical history. Would you describe her as having been a healthy woman, on the whole?'

'We're talking about physical health?'

'The complete spectrum.'

'I'm not quite clear what you mean by that, but in general terms she . . . She's in good physical shape, yes.'

'Didn't she suffer an illness of some kind, about three years ago?'

'Three years?' I frowned.

'According to your daughter Deborah, she was hit rather badly by . . .' Picking up the typed sheet of paper, Sinclair brought it closer to his eyes. '*Polymyalgia rheumatica*. A very painful condition, with symptoms not unlike acute arthritis.'

'Oh — that's right.' I had almost forgotten. 'She was in a lot of discomfort for a while. But the doctor gave her tablets which took the pain right away, and I don't think she's been troubled with it since.'

'That apart, she's had no other complaint?'

'Not that I'm aware of. Did Deborah mention anything else?'

'No, she didn't.' The Inspector sat motionless, as if brooding. 'Now, Mr Brent, a trickier question. What can you tell me about your wife's mental state?'

'I guessed we'd be getting to that. If it's a clinical report you're after . . .'

'What I'm after is your own assessment. You've been living with her: you must have formed some view of her behaviour. Was she prone to depression, hysteria — anything of that nature?'

'What does Deborah say?'

'I wish you'd stop referring everything to your daughter. It's you I'm asking.'

'Sorry. I just had this stupid idea you were placing more weight on her opinions than mine. For what it's worth, my answer is that I've never gained the impression of abnormal moodiness on Sara's part. The reverse, if anything. She's always been rather placid, easy-going. As I've already said, she seemed perfectly content in a domestic environment. If she ever got depressed . . . She disguised it remarkably well, that's all I can say.'

'No history of depressive illness in her family?'

'Again, not to the best of my knowledge.'

I sat waiting. He was humming once more under his breath. After a lengthy interval I asked, 'Is that everything?'

Swivelling his chair, he brought his silhouette out of profile and gazed at me intently. 'Let's now go back again to Sunday morning. Describe all that happened.'

The noise I made was beyond exasperation. 'How many times?' I implored, beating the air. 'You must have a dozen sets of notes about it already. What possible purpose—'

'Just tell me again.'

Against the odds, I re-established self-governance of my voice. I spoke slowly and precisely. 'At about ten-fifteen I was in the living-room, reading the Sunday papers. Sara called from the hall that she was going for a walk. I said all right, and was there anything to be done? No, she said. The street door—'

'Not feeling energetic yourself?'

'Beg pardon?'

'You didn't suggest going with her?'

'No. I wanted to relax.'

'But the weather was glorious. And from what I can make out, a walk in the streets involving your wife was quite an event. I'd have thought you might have felt inclined to go along too.'

'It never occurred to me,' I said briefly. 'Shall I go on?'

'Please.'

'I heard the street door close. After that I lost track of the time; probably dozed off. It wasn't—'

'That a habit of yours? Falling asleep in the morning?'

'I'd had a hectic week, and I hadn't been sleeping well.'

'Oh? Things on your mind?'

'The self-employed usually have.'

'But do you always sleep badly? You talk as if last week was exceptional.'

For a moment I closed my eyes. 'I don't make a practice of monitoring my slumber processes. I'm simply telling you what I can remember. On Sunday morning I was tired, I felt like a rest. My wife went for a stroll, I stayed home. Is that too humdrum for you?'

'Not for me,' he said obliquely. 'Carry on. Having slept, you woke about twelve-thirty or soon after, to find the house still empty. You went outside, saw your wife's coat on the telephone stand, so you assumed—'

'I saw a coat. Deborah has since told me it was hers.'

'Ah. That's right. You don't take much interest in what the various members of your family are wearing?'

'I'm a bit vague about clothes, as such. As for taking no interest—'

'Too preoccupied with business affairs, perhaps?'

'As it happens, I do have weightier matters to think about than the family taste in fashions. Could you describe your wife's wardrobe?'

'Quite a slice of it. But then,' he added with an air of tolerance, 'I'm a trained cop, aren't I? Taught to assimilate such things, regardless of whether it's someone close to me or not.'

'You seem to be implying that I'm not particularly close to my wife.'

'I do?'

'Either that, or . . .'

'Or what, Mr Brent?'

Not for the first time, a weird sensation began to crawl over me. It was as though I were trapped inside a vast honeycomb structure incorporating endless sidetracks, into which I was repeatedly being diverted. As in a dream, there was no rational sequence to the pattern. I kept stumbling along, knowing that the direction was wrong but powerless to correct the error. Through the gloom, I stared at Sinclair with a mute loathing that was real and unrehearsed. Seemingly oblivious, he hauled me back adroitly, yet again, to the main shaft.

'Let's return, shall we, to the morning in question. Having spotted the coat, you went through to the kitchen . . .'

'I found the roast lamb practically on fire in the oven. Then the girls came home and we all got very anxious. Carol and I drove around the streets, looking for my wife. Telephoned various people. Finally I rang through here.'

'As anybody would have done,' he said on a sudden note of grave commiseration. 'Especially with a pair of agitated daughters to consider. Been out, hadn't they, all morning? Carol helping the curate. Deborah with her literary pals.'

'Right,' I said, as he paused apparently for confirmation.

'Both long-standing arrangements, these?'

'It wasn't a regular—'

'I mean, in each case it was fixed up a day or two previously? They weren't sudden, off-the-cuff decisions?'

'I believe not.'

'So your wife would have known that both girls would be out of the house that morning?'

'Presumably.'

He whistled a few soft notes. 'For that matter, so would you?'

'If I'd borne it particularly in mind.'

'Are you saying you didn't?'

I moved restively. 'As far as I can recall, I was dimly aware that Carol was involved with something going on at the church. Also, I think I knew that Deborah and her pals had some play-writing project in hand. Altogether, I wasn't amazed when they both went out. Let's put it that way.'

'Fine. Let me put it this way. It was known to you beforehand that, apart from yourself and your wife, the house would be empty on Sunday morning. Any argument about that?'

'Maybe not, except that I can't see it's relevant.'

'Bear with me, please,' he said politely. 'I'm trying to build up a picture. Talking of pictures . . . Your son Peter was away in France, so that took care of him, didn't it?'

'I don't understand the insinuation.'

'What I'm suggesting, Mr Brent, is that you might have anticipated the chance of . . . shall we say, a heart-to-heart talk with your wife? After all, you had plenty to discuss.'

'I've no idea what you mean.'

'Come on. You're heavily entangled with two other young women at the office. For all I know, one or both of them could be piling on the pressure. Or, you could have been getting itchy feet yourself. Either way, if that's not a reason for thrashing things out with your wife . . .'

'You've got a damn nerve. Putting two and two together and making a thousand.'

'It's our trade,' he said regretfully. 'Disproving the laws of mathematics. You'd be surprised how flexible they are.'

'This time your figures have gone berserk. There was no chat between my wife and me. The need hadn't arisen. I've told you quite frankly, I've always kept my escapades hidden from her.'

'Enjoyed a good few, have you, sir?'

I spent a few moments simmering. 'Since you ask, I'll admit I'm a susceptible type of guy and I may have kicked over the traces once or twice too often . . . but I've not let it hurt Sara. She's never had the slightest cause to suspect, so phut goes your discussion theory.'

'What makes you so positive she never suspected?'

'As the chap who's been living with her, I ought to know.'

'Yes,' he said, without intonation, 'you ought. You're saying, then, you didn't have anything out with her on Sunday morning?'

'There was nothing to *have out*.'

'Right. I'll accept that. On the other hand,' he went on, as I started to relax, 'we're still left with a situation where you'd conceivably be under pressure from outside sources to disturb the status quo: which could have a bearing on what we're talking about. Are you with me?'

'Nowhere near.'

'I take leave to doubt that.'

An incredulous laugh forced its way out of my throat. 'You're the limit. You talk in half-baked riddles, then have the gall to expect people to come back with considered replies. Is this all you're capable of?'

His silence had the effect of making my words echo and re-echo, until the resonances expired and the beating of the rain against the panes returned to dominate. Beneath the window, Merton sat as immovably as his chief, ballpoint poised above pad. I wondered whether our exchange was there in ink, verbatim or summarized; or whether his apparent scribblings were a bluff. At this stage, nothing seemed too improbable to dismiss. The pair of them were playing some game of their own, and I wasn't in on the rules.

Which needn't prevent me, I reasoned, from organizing a counter-attraction. Rising, I said with finality, 'Now, if you've no objection, I think I'll be off. Any further questions can wait until I've taken legal advice. You know where to find me.'

Neither of them stirred or spoke as I walked out of the room.

CHAPTER ELEVEN

I was halfway home before I remembered I had failed to ask Sinclair about the possibility of invoking Interpol's aid to locate Peter.

The trauma of his interrogation had driven it out of my mind. There was nothing for it but to telephone the Bardeau household yet again, and this time, I swore to myself, my approach would be uncompromising. The time had come to end this nonsense. If they still could tell me nothing, I should have to insist upon more concrete measures. Peter's reappearance was vital.

The Rev. Lionel Gooch was with Carol on the living-room sofa. Recoiling at the door, I said, 'Where's Debbie?'

Carol looked through me. The curate said kindly, 'Hi, Mr Brent. Debbie's around. I think I heard her go upstairs.'

His right arm was around the back of Carol's neck; the fingers of that hand were dangling limply in the region of the front of her sweater. Muttering thanks, I withdrew and reached the foot of the stairs before pausing, demanding of myself what I was thanking him for, why I didn't go back inside and tell him to get out, stay out. I felt starved and weak. On shaky legs, I climbed the staircase and knocked at Debbie's bedroom door. There was no reply.

A sound reached me from behind the door that led to Sara's dressmaking room. Seeing that it was ajar, I shoved it open. With her back to me, Debbie was standing at the worktable, sifting through documents. She turned her head.

'Just got back?'

'This minute.' I went inside, closed the door. 'Sorry to be so long.'

Absent-mindedly she glanced at her watch. 'I'd lost track of the time. Did the Inspector tell you anything?'

'He asked plenty. Put me through the mangle.' I leaned against the worktable. 'Routine, I suppose.'

'They have to ask questions.' Her voice was listless, as if she had undergone some vast though not unexpected disappointment. I nodded at the documents.

'Anything?'

'I thought there might be some mention of the people she's dealt with. But it's mostly figures and materials. Here and there it refers to a Mrs C. or a Miss W., but that's all.'

'So none of it's any help?'

With a shake of the head she swept the papers back into a drawer, closed it, stood eyeing me more closely. 'Anyway, if there had been anything, the police would have spotted it. Dad, you look terrible. Have you eaten?'

'Not since lunch.' I sat heavily on an ottoman by the wall. 'I'll have something presently. First, Debbie, I'd like a word. It's about Sunday.' Hesitating over an approach shot, I changed my mind and drove straight for the pin. 'Exactly when did you tell your mother you'd be spending the morning with Maureen and Brenda?'

'Half an hour before I went. Why?'

'Was that the first she knew of it?'

'Oh no. I'd mentioned it back in the week. She knew I was planning to go. Is it important?'

I had the feeling she asked the question to see what I thought, not because the possible significance had escaped her. I said evasively, 'It's just one of the points

Sinclair raised. What about Carol?'

'What about her?'

'Her stint at the church was prearranged, too?'

'Yes. Lionel called on Thursday to ask if she could help.'

'Called here?'

'Telephoned, I mean. Dad, come downstairs to the kitchen. I'll scramble you some eggs . . .'

'Wait a bit.' I intercepted her by the door. 'Let's get this quite straight. Your mother was in no doubt that you'd both be out of the house on Sunday morning: is that correct?'

'Yes, I'd say so.' Debbie became very still. 'You're thinking she might have been—'

'I'm doing my best to keep an open mind. One more question. How about me? Should I have been aware of the arrangements?'

She blinked. 'Don't you remember?'

'I'm not sure.' I leaned against the door. The way I was feeling, any available support was welcome; besides which, the odd look in Debbie's eyes seemed to underline my need for material backing.

She said, 'Did Inspector Sinclair ask you that, this evening?'

'There weren't many questions he forgot. The point is, I honestly can't decide whether I knew or not . . .'

'I don't see that it matters.'

'It *could* matter. Taken along with the photograph—'

'Don't be silly. No point in pursuing that.'

'But don't you see? I was in the house with her that morning. I could have prevented her going out. Or I could have gone with her. So what did I do instead? Sat there like a lump of lard while she slid out of our lives. Can you blame me for questioning myself, wondering if I could have—'

'Dad!' Gripping my arms, she shook me hard. 'You're not

doing any good. Nobody's psychic. If anyone's at fault . . .'
She stumbled over her phrases. 'We could just as easily . . .
Carol and I . . . there was no need . . .'

Although she had stopped shaking me, she clung on to
my arms, and I heard her give a single, stifled sob and a
gasp. For a few seconds we remained in contact; then,
aware of a slight stiffening of her body, I let her disengage
herself, which she did jerkily, like someone feeling her
way backwards through a hedge. When I spoke again, it
was on a clumsily lighter note.

'The self-condemnation syndrome, I guess they'd call
it. Hits most people in our position, and achieves
nothing.'

'Only if it helps to get someone back.' Tweaking a
handkerchief from her sleeve, she dabbed swiftly at her
eyes, blew her nose. 'And makes them more appreciated
when they are.'

'Speaking for myself, I don't think I've ever lacked
appreciation of your mother's qualities.'

'But did she know that?'

'Well, I hope so. What more could I have—'

'You might have taken more notice of her.' Suddenly,
Debbie was on the attack.

'I wasn't aware . . .'

'Exactly! You never did seem to be aware. Just drifted
on in your own way, leaving her to . . . Oh, forget it.'
Stuffing the handkerchief viciously back into its sleeve,
she reached for the door-handle. I seized her wrist.

'A moment ago,' I pointed out, 'we agreed it was no use
allocating blame. Now, you seem to be pinning it firmly
to me. Well, okay. You could be right. What do you want
me to do about it, specifically, this minute?'

'Since you ask,' she said, low-voiced, 'for a start, you
could try calling it a day with that floozie of yours at the
office.'

An element of restraint was discernible in Madame Bardeau's otherwise warm and sympathetic delivery. 'Certainly, Mr Brent. We very well comprehend your emotions—your feelings, and we are doing all that we can. You know, it's our daughter also. We are just as concerned as you.'

'So you are getting a little anxious?'

I heard her take a quick breath. 'Not about their safety. Nat-ur-ally, we should like the police to find them as soon as possible. We feel deeply for you in your position.'

'Are you having radio messages put out?'

'We have suggested it to the police. I think so, yes. The Prefect in control of the area . . .'

I listened restlessly while she eulogized the local force, cutting in as soon as I decently could. 'Is it possible for me to speak directly with the Prefect?'

'I can perhaps tell you the number,' she said, after a pause. 'Unfortunately you will learn very little more—'

'Will you give it to me, please?'

Forbearingly she spelt it out. Thanking her, I tried hurriedly to make it clear that my persistence was no reflection upon her or her husband, to which she replied graciously that she understood to perfection and hoped I would have some luck. When I rang the number she had given me, I was connected with an Inspector Durell, whose English had never thrown off a limp. By the time I had identified myself and conveyed the gist of what I was after, his already brittle patience had thinned to vanishing point. The search, he gave me peremptorily to understand, was being conducted with thoroughness the most enormous over an area the most extensive, at a pace the most pressing consistent with a proper prudence. Any positive news would be instantly conveyed. At the present time, there was nothing more to be done.

'An aerial search?' I suggested.

He spluttered over the line. In the midst of what
seemed to be an explanation of the limits to their
resources, I interrupted him without ceremony. 'If they're
not found by tomorrow, I'm coming over there myself to
stir things up. You tell that to your boss.'

Dropping the receiver with considerable noise, I
glanced round to find the Rev. Lionel Gooch at my
elbow. 'Trouble with the Frogs?' he enquired
sympathetically. 'Sounds like you're having the devil of a
time. If there's anything I can do . . .'

'Can you look into a crystal ball and find people?'

'Never tried,' he said sunnily. He followed me along the
hall to the street door and out into the porch, where I
turned to confront him. I spoke bluntly.

'You're fond of Carol?'

'Yes, very. She's a sweet kid.'

'You know she's just sixteen, and still at school?'

He regarded me with a faint smile. 'We're not having a
fling, Mr Brent, if that's what you're implying. Carol's
interested in the church and she helps us a lot. So I'm
trying to be some help in return, that's all. Would you
sooner I didn't call?'

I muttered something about not wanting to deprive
Carol of understanding companionship when she needed
it most. 'At the moment, she doesn't respond to me,' I
explained, hearing and detesting the whine in my voice. 'I
get the feeling she rather holds me responsible for her
mother's disappearance.'

'I'm sure you're wrong.' His eyes bulged at me from
close range. 'Emotionally speaking, she's been knocked
edgewise, I'd say. Right now, what she needs is an
outsider. That's all I am. As a churchman, I've known
Carol for a couple of years and she may well have some
romantic notions about me, but frankly, sir, I'm
detached. I do in fact have a steady relationship with
someone else. Our deputy organist, Miss Chandler.

Maybe you've met her? No, of course you wouldn't have. Anyway, I hope that's clarified the position. I'd hate to add to your worries at such a time.'

The words were fine. I was less charmed by his utterance of them: they added up to what sounded like a prepared speech. Taking the easy path, however, I received them at face value and even managed a thin smile. 'That does reassure me. Sorry if I spoke out of turn.' He brandished a forgiving arm. 'Just one other thing,' I added, as he turned to leave. 'Has Carol . . . er, spoken to you any more about the photo?'

'The one of your wife? We've discussed it, sure.'

'And Carol seems genuinely convinced it's a good likeness?'

'Right. But I wouldn't read too much into that, Mr Brent. I've done some camerawork myself. I know how prints can distort and how people's reactions to them can vary. It's a shot of her mother, okay? So naturally Carol sees it that way. She can't understand—'

'Our difference of opinion,' I said wearily, 'goes a little further than that.'

'Sure it does. But it doesn't affect what I'm saying. You know, about a year back I took a picture of a group of our church ladies on the Sundries Stall at the summer fête, and when I showed it afterwards to the vicar he maintained . . . he *insisted* that one of them in the centre was a Mrs Worth, who runs the Sewing Guild; whereas I knew, and everyone else knew, that it was actually a Miss Spencer, who sees to Floral Decorations. Not only that: it was common knowledge that Mrs Worth had been on holiday in Majorca at the time. And yet despite this, for quite a while nothing would shift him. He saw it as Mrs Worth—that was it. He even refused to use the picture in that month's church magazine, although Miss Spencer identified herself and everyone else confirmed it. And he's not normally an obstinate man. He just had this conviction that couldn't be shaken. See what I mean?'

'It's not quite the same. In this instance, it's Carol's mother and my wife.'

Gooch examined me keenly. 'You've not been married before, Mr Brent?'

'Sorry, no. Nothing like that.'

'Eyesight? You wear glasses for reading?'

I shook my head.

'Contact lenses? If you wore a pair of the flexible type and they'd become distorted . . .'

'There's nothing wrong with my vision. I don't use any artificial aids. The police and I have been into all that.'

'Well . . . does Carol wear lenses, perhaps?'

'None of us do. You can forget that angle.'

'Puzzling,' he murmured, teetering on the porch-edge. Now that the subject had arisen, he seemed unwilling to let it sink back out of sight. 'Can you say in what details the photograph differs from your own conception of your wife's face?'

'It's just a different shape. Heavier, more . . . more rounded. That's not quite the word. Puffier. The eyes are smaller.'

'Is that all?'

'It's not the face of the woman I'm familiar with. Now you'll have to excuse me, Mr Gooch. I've things to see to.'

'Yes,' he said with an air of sincerity, 'I know you're a busy man at the best of times. Carol tells me you've generally got a fair bit on your plate.'

The call-box at the corner, to my relief, was vacant and in service. I had brought along a supply of coins. Eleanor answered promptly. 'Hullo, my pet. You're on an outside line?'

'I thought it might be safer. The cops seem to be watching my movements. They could be tapping my phone, for all I know.'

'How dramatic. Why would they want to do that?'

'You tell me. But having had the full treatment down at the station this evening . . . Linny, they know about us. We've been seen together.'

'Aren't they the smart little ferrets?' she said coolly. 'Not surprising, though, when you think about it. With all this talk of yours about wrong snapshots, you must have quickened their curiosity. Does it change anything?'

'It means they're inclined to treat everything I say as if I'd jerked the pin out of a grenade.'

'Don't tell me they're accusing you of anything?'

'I'm not quite certain. All Sinclair does is drop weighty hints. He seems to have the fixed idea that I wanted Sara out of the way.'

'Well, didn't you?'

'Don't be ridiculous. Of course,' I added hastily, 'I'd have liked the path to be clear for us, but that's hardly . . .' I paused. 'You don't really imagine I'd anything to do with it?'

'Ralphie-Boo, you're scarcely the type. I don't see you consciously doing anything so decisive.'

'Thanks. Unconsciously?'

Her dual-tone laugh tolled in my ear. 'I'm no mind-reader, cherub. Who knows what inner turbulence I could have unleashed? You must admit, this identity-block you seem to be experiencing has some intriguing overtones, but when it comes to causes and effects . . . Just watch your step, that's my advice. If you do know anything, over and above what you've told me, keep it to yourself. Let them make the running. That way, nobody can . . . Hullo, hullo!'

'What is it?' I said, alarmed.

'A police car's just stopped outside.'

'In the drive?'

'Not among the azaleas, my sweet. A burly uniformed figure is climbing out. He's clumping up to the front door. I wonder what he's after?'

'Don't tell him anything, Linny.'

'But they already know. According to you.'

'I mean, stick to the basic facts. It's just been an office liaison, nothing heavy—okay?'

'Don't panic. I shan't embroider. I'd better go and answer the door. Talk to you later.'

I hung up, sweating. Sinclair had evidently wasted little time. Having made a start on the knot, he had got interested and was now plucking busily at the various strands, experimenting to see how it unravelled. I tried putting myself in his place. What questions would I ask Eleanor? Anything that might remotely be relevant. In her position, how would I answer? Cannily.

Luckily, I could trust Eleanor. She had her own interests to protect.

On the other hand, if Sinclair were to turn on the heat . . .

Snatching up the receiver, I dialled another number. The ringing tone bleeped endlessly. In despair, I was about to hang up when a man's voice answered. I thrust in more money. 'Is it possible to speak to Miss Harwood?'

'Who's calling?' The voice was friendly, working-class, anxious to oblige.

'My name's Ralph Brent. I'm Miss Harwood's—'

'Oh, Mr. Brent. My daughter's spoken a lot about you. Nice to make your acquaintance after all this time. Not acquaintance exactly, ha ha. Sort of verbal contact, you might say. Very happy, she is, working with you. She was telling us . . . Excuse me, I mustn't blather on. Did you want to talk to her?'

'If it's convenient,' I croaked.

'Hold on a minute. Chrissie! Your boss wants you. On her way, Mr Brent. Drying her hair, she was. Here she is now. Nice to have spoken with you. There you are, love, don't keep Mr Brent waiting, he's in a call-box . . .'

Tina said breathlessly, 'H'llo?'

'Is your father still there, or can you talk?'

'He's on his way back to the lounge. All right now. What's the matter? Has your wife turned up?'

'No, but I'll tell you who might turn up any minute— at your place. The police.'

'*Police*? Why here?'

'They know about you and me. I can't explain now, but I think I'm under suspicion and they may very well want to ask you some questions about our . . . relationship. I thought I should warn you.'

'I see. You want me to say nothing?'

'That won't do much good. You'll have to admit we've been seeing each other, but ask them to keep it confidential: I'm sure they'll agree to. If nothing gets out . . .'

'Wait a minute, Ralph. Isn't this just what we've been waiting for?'

'Come again?'

'Don't you remember? This afternoon, when I suggested using this to bring things to a head, you said to give it a few days longer. Well, there's no point now, is there? The police know. And your wife's still missing, so it looks as if she's not coming back. Sooner or later there'd have to be a bust-up—why not make it now?'

'That's impossible, Tina.'

'Why is it?'

'Surely you can see. If I were to choose this moment to run off with you, all the official suspicions would be confirmed. They'd assume I'd bumped my wife off to leave ourselves a clear field.'

'But you haven't,' she said reasonably. 'So what difference does it make?'

'Suppose they were to find her body?'

'You think she might have been killed?'

'I don't *know*, Tina. How can I possibly say? Anything could have happened to her. One of the possibilities is that she's dead, and if that's the case then I'm a suspect. Can't you see that?'

'You'd soon be able to prove you hadn't done it.'

'How?'

'Your movements wouldn't fit, would they? Once the police started investigating . . .'

The pips intruded. Swearing, I crammed more coins into the slot, restoring the connection in time to hear, '. . . wouldn't add up, and they'd have to try elsewhere, so there'd be no—'

'You're taking a rather airy view of the whole thing, Tina. It mightn't be so simple. What if my movements did happen to fit, near enough? Or there was insufficient proof, one way or the other? What if I was accused of hiring someone to put her out of the way?'

'It's all ifs,' she said petulantly. 'Not likely to happen, is it? You're just raising difficulties. Don't you *want* us to be together, Ralph?'

'Darling, of course I do.' My mind raced desperately. 'But not in these circumstances. Give it a few days—'

'You keep saying that. Days, weeks, months. How much longer?'

'You've got to understand my position . . .'

'I just wish I did. I can't make out whether you want to leave your family or not. Ralph . . .'

'Yes, what is it?'

'You haven't really done anything to your wife, have you? Is this why you're so jumpy?'

'For God's sake,' I said furiously. 'How can you even suggest such a thing?'

'Well, if it's not that, then I don't understand. You're behaving stupidly. If the police come, I shall tell them everything and I shan't care if my parents hear, either. I'll spread it all around. Then we'll see what happens, won't we?'

Her receiver slammed down. Searching for more

change, I found that I had inserted my final 10p. For a second or two I rested my head against the door-frame; then I left the call-box. It was starting to rain again.

CHAPTER TWELVE

You haven't really done anything to your wife, have you?

Mechanically stepping over the puddles, I re-examined the question as it tramped noisily through my brain. Nothing I could do would send it away. And each time it came back it was stronger, more insistent, like an impudent child emboldened by adult uncertainty. *Is this why you're so jumpy?*

Surely I had a right to be jumpy? A missing wife was no sedative. Anyone in my position would have felt the same. *You've got to understand my position.*

To whom, precisely, had I been addressing that remark? To Tina, as an admonition? Or to myself, as a reminder?

A reminder of what?

As I turned the corner into my own street, I spotted the car. It was one of many that were parked for the night on the verges; but it was different. When I left the house, it had been stationed fifty yards away with a couple of heads visible inside. Now, it was just beyond the junction from which I was emerging, and the heads were still in evidence although the faces were looking studiously the opposite way.

My initial anger yielded to contempt. A manpower problem? They seemed to be bringing it on themselves. If they were determined to track every move I made, even when it was on foot, that was their headache.

Hard on the heels of the contempt came funk. The

police *were* undermanned: everyone said so. And yet for some reason they were finding the resources to keep me under surveillance, twenty-four hours a day. Why? What were they hoping to discover?

If the police come, I shall tell them everything. I'll spread it all around.

Assuming the threat was not an idle one, I was done for. Eleanor would learn of my involvement with Tina: in her wrath, she would sell me to the tax authorities. She had as good as said so, and I believed her.

I walked on slowly towards the house, fighting the urge to glance back.

What else had Eleanor said?

I can't see you consciously doing anything so decisive.

How much had I been conscious of on Sunday morning? Between the time when I dozed off and the time when I came round, a two-hour expanse of utter oblivion lay beyond my ability to chart. I had fallen asleep in a chair and I had regained my senses in the same chair: in the interim . . .

Who knows what inner turbulence I could have unleashed?

Two hours. An eye-blink; an eternity. In a hundred and twenty minutes, a motorist could drive from London to Birmingham. Concorde could cross most of the Atlantic. Two of Brahms's symphonies could be played, with time to spare. A person could vanish.

Don't tell me they're accusing you of something?

Passing the Freebody house, I kept my gaze rigidly ahead in case either of them was at a window, poised to catch my eye. An improbable occurrence, but I didn't want to meet anyone, least of all a Freebody. The car to my rear, my ears informed me, had remained stationary. There was no reason why it shouldn't, since its occupants had a clear view. They were waiting to see whether I turned in.

A man of persistence, Inspector Sinclair. Obsessed with the idea that I had wanted Sara out of the way.

Well, didn't you?

It wasn't true. Apart from the desire, I lacked the mentality, the resolution. The ruthlessness.

Well, if it's not that, then I don't understand . . .

By-passing the street door, I took the side gate to the back of the house and, standing on the edge of the patio, stared across the lawn at the trees and shrubs whose outlines were starting to blur in the dusk and drizzle. By my watch, it was nine-twenty. At this hour on recent evenings, the daylight had barely been impaired. Just last week, Sara had been out there nightly until ten, trimming and weeding. Less assiduously, Debbie had lent a hand. From the window of what I termed my study—an over-sized cupboard between living-room and kitchen—I had been able to watch them in an unseeing kind of way while going through the firm's accounts. My conscience had been clear. Sara, I knew, liked to be left alone to get on with it. As for Debbie, she seemed to welcome the exercise.

Watching in the gloom, I could almost persuade myself that Sara was visible now, wielding an implement on the vegetable patch beyond its protective hedge. A trick of the eyes. Helped, naturally, by an overheated brain, still running in overdrive after a pair of fraught telephone conversations. It was because of this mental hyperactivity that I was delaying my return indoors. When I met the girls again, I wanted to be well in command of myself.

Taking out the pack of cigarettes I kept pocketed as a precaution, I stuck one between my lips and struck a match. As the tiny flare subsided, the impression of movement behind the hedge faded too. I stood exhaling smoke, contemplating the stillness.

Once more the drizzle was easing. Overhead, a winking

red light travelled serenely across the sky, bound for
Heathrow.

Presently I stepped on to the wet grass and sauntered
towards the gap in the hedge. As I approached, I caught
the faintest of sounds, as if a couple of small pebbles had
slithered and collided.

I slowed further. Three yards from the gap, I came to a
standstill. To my right, the height of the hedge was
augmented by a clump of mixed trees, mainly conifers:
the stony clink seemed to have come from there. I stood
motionless. Nothing stirred.

'Anyone there?'

The sharp reediness of my own voice startled me. It
seemed to have no other effect. Taking a few more steps,
I stationed myself almost in the centre of the gap, trying
to think of something else to say that wouldn't brand me
as an idiot. From the vicinity of the conifers came a
distinct rustling, the sound of an impact: a gasp. Darting
across, I hoisted a prone figure to its knees.

'Debbie—it's you! What in hell are you up to?'

Detaching herself from me, she rose the rest of the way
to her feet and stood off a little, rubbing her left cheek
with one hand while dusting herself down with the other.
She wore jeans and an anorak. On the ground nearby lay
a garden shovel with mud clinging to its blade. I looked
from it back to her with a sense of mounting bewilder-
ment.

'You're not gardening at a time like this?'

'Why not?' Uncovering her cheek, she inspected her
fingers. 'I wanted something to do.'

An abrasion across the cheekbone suggested that she
had walked into an overhanging branch. I passed her a
handkerchief. Taking it silently, she began dabbing at
the tender area while I divided my attention between her,
the shovel, and a mound of newly-turned earth next to a
sizable crater alongside a row of peas.

'Do?' I echoed. 'Surely you've enough on your plate, without digging holes and getting drenched to the skin? What possessed you to come out here?'

She said woodenly, 'You seem to be getting around quite a bit. Why shouldn't I?'

'Come back indoors, sweetheart. Let's put a dressing on that graze, get you dried off.'

She stayed where she was. As if linked by a guide-wire, we both glanced at the area of upturned soil: it seemed to have been excavated at random, without plan or method. I looked back at her. 'Why dig around here, like this? What the blazes do you think you're up to?'

'Maybe you can enlighten us too, Miss Brent.'

Debbie jumped violently as I whirled. The voice had spoken from the hedge-space, where the incontestable figure of Detective-Constable Merton stood alongside that of a young female colleague: both were observing us. I could think of nothing less trite to say than, 'What are you doing here?'

He advanced to join us. 'Not ideal gardening weather,' he remarked, looking down at the upheaval. 'Somebody must be keen.'

'If it's any business of yours,' Debbie said tartly, 'I felt like some exercise. So I decided to dig for a while, that's all.'

'I'd have thought,' Merton said mildly, 'a walk or a jog, on a night like this.' Moving closer, he peered at her cheek. Debbie retreated a pace.

'I did this by walking into a tree. What are you all staring at me for?'

'Sweetheart,' I said, 'nobody's trying to—'

'Don't call me that.'

Merton and his companion swapped glances. I rounded on them. 'Whether or not it was your intention, you've got her pretty upset. By what right can you invade private property and snoop on people?'

My words seemed to bounce off their ears and fade into the gathering night. Returning to the excavations, Merton stood pondering them for a space. 'A bit late,' he suggested, 'for potatoes. Drainage? But you can't have a flood problem here. It's all on the level.' He glanced round. 'The terrain, I'm talking about.'

Debbie said, 'I'm going indoors.'

Holding the handkerchief to her cheek, she circumnavigated the three of us and headed off through the gap. Merton's associate, a dark-haired young woman with hips, called after her, 'Use some antiseptic.'

Catching her eye, Merton jerked his chin. With a nod, she went after Debbie across the lawn. Fighting a sense of unreality, I watched them enter the house together, saw the kitchen light snap on, before turning back to the detective. 'What would you like me to do? Stay here, go there? Just let me know what you have in mind.'

'It's your garden.'

'Yes? You could have fooled me.'

He spoke in a confidential undertone. 'Between ourselves, Mr Brent . . . why do *you* think your daughter was digging here?'

'Between ourselves, what possible concern is it of yours?'

Making a sudden dive, he grabbed up the shovel and began to examine it minutely. 'Fond of gardening, your daughter?'

'She helps out.'

His gaze roamed. 'A lot of work,' he said knowingly. 'This time of year, especially. Grass to keep down, borders to trim. Your lawn, if you'll pardon my saying so, looks as if it could use a shave.'

'We've not had a great deal of spare time, just lately.'

'No, I can imagine. And yet young Deborah seems to have found an hour or two to dig out a fairly meaningless few hundredweight of topsoil and scatter it all over the place. Funny, that.'

I faced him squarely. 'Just what are you saying, Merton?'

Instead of replying, he looked down at the shovel he was clasping. 'Mind if I use this?'

Without bothering to await an answer, he peeled off his jacket and set to work. Watching the inaccurate but lusty thrusts of the blade, I felt fear seep like chilled syrup into every part of me. Events seemed to be pushing on, out of control, towards a conclusion which, although common knowledge to everyone else, remained an enigma to me. Having taken the crater's perimeter up to the edge of the peas, Merton started to go deeper. Now and then, an impact announced a collision between the blade and something more solid than soil; each time, he paused to examine the spot before digging on. Mounds of subsoil added themselves to the growing rampart. After a while I said from my spectator standpoint, 'Just how deep are you planning to go?'

Taking a few breaths, he glanced up at me in silence and then got down to it again. By now the crater was two or three feet deep in places and the shovel was biting into clay: I could hear the duller note of each contact, although in the failing light it was becoming hard to see. Before long, Merton leaned the shovel carefully to one side and clambered a little stiffly out of the pit. Straightening his back with caution, he shifted some damp hair out of his eyes.

'Mind leading the way back to the house, sir?'

'I do, actually. I'd much prefer it if you found your own way off the premises. The pair of you. By what right —'

'Save the speeches,' he advised tiredly, massaging his palms. 'We're all familiar with the script. Rights? So far, everything I've done has been with your consent. You want to alter that? Start raising objections? It's up to you.'

'What I want, is to know what this is all about.'

'Ah,' he said, sounding more animated. 'Wouldn't we all?'

Debbie, with a plaster on her cheek and pulled-back hair that gave her a slightly staring-eyed look, was drinking coffee with the woman detective at the kitchen table when we rejoined them. She made more, and the four of us sat silently sipping, like survivors from a battlefield. Nobody seemed inclined to talk.

I realized I was famished. Finding the biscuit tin, I offered it round: nobody accepted. The crunching sounds I proceeded to make were clearly audible, but I no longer cared. Debbie sat facing partly away from me, apparently intent upon the design of the cooker. Swallowing the final crumb, I glanced at her profile.

'Carol okay?'

She nodded.

'Did you dose her up again?'

Another nod. Merton looked up from his cup. 'Keeping her sedated?'

'The quack advised it.'

He swapped another glance with his colleague, who had lively, good-natured eyes. Now that I saw her under a light, I discovered that her hair was more coppery than dark. She looked embarrassed. Seemingly immune to atmosphere, Merton saucered his cup with a clatter and leaned back in his chair, flexing his wrists. 'Not used to manual labour,' he observed humorously. 'How about you, Deborah? Got any muscular aches or pains?'

'If you've any more questions to put to my daughter,' I said, 'I'll have to insist—'

'It's no use going on at me.' She inserted the remark with a chilling deftness. 'I'm not saying any more.'

Merton contemplated the ceiling. 'I'd like you both,' he said presently, 'to be here tomorrow morning, between nine and ten. In the meantime, I don't want any more agricultural activities undertaken, of any kind. That understood?'

I pushed the biscuit tin aside. 'We'll do as we damn well please.'

He whistled in a pained way between his teeth. 'Not constructive, Mr Brent. Not helpful at all. Neither is it practical.'

'What you're saying is, we're going to be under surveillance inside our own property?'

'I'm saying . . .'

His voice slurred off as the telephone rang in the hall. I leapt up. 'Excuse me. I take it I'm still allowed to answer my own calls?'

He made no comment. Closing the kitchen door behind me, I lifted the receiver and said softly, 'Yes?' I was expecting to hear Eleanor's voice. *Talk to you later*, she had said. The earpiece, however, remained mute. I tried again. 'Hullo?'

I recited the number. A click or two was chased by a further silence, then the faintest of voices, the ghostliest shadow of human articulation, like a recording being played back with the needle partly out of the groove. I pressed a finger into my other ear. 'What's that? Can you speak up, please?'

'Peter. I can't . . .'

A rushing noise encroached on the line. Frantically I rattled the receiver rest. 'Hullo! Are you there? Pete—is that you?'

The noise expired in another click, and the line went dead.

CHAPTER THIRTEEN

Merton emerged from the kitchen to gaze at me. 'Your son?'

'He's been cut off.' I pounded the telephone stand. 'Hullo? Anyone there?'

'Hang up. He'll come through again.'

Notwithstanding its source, the counsel had its merits. Replacing the receiver with reluctance, I stood glaring down at it. 'I heard him . . . just for a second. No mistaking his voice.'

'Well, that's something.' Merton's inspection of me was quizzical. 'One load off your mind, at least.'

'Damn Continental telephones.' In frustration I stamped up and down the hall. 'The entire system's a disaster. The trouble I've had—'

'Could be the fault of British Telecom,' he pointed out.

'Care to take a bet? Over there, they make a hash of everything. Three days to trace four youngsters on a camping trip! It's scandalous.'

We stood watching the telephone.

'If we go back to the kitchen,' suggested Merton, 'it'll ring again.'

We went back to the kitchen.

Debbie said, 'Was it Peter?'

I nodded. 'He got cut off.'

The four of us sat listening.

'Could be pressure,' Merton observed, 'on the overseas exchange. Once lose your place in the queue . . .'

Debbie stood up. 'I'd better look in on Carol.'

When she was out of the room, I said, 'How long do the two of you plan to stay here?'

'We'll stick around,' Merton replied calmly, 'till Peter

calls back. If you've no objection.'

With a disdainful laugh I turned to his colleague. 'Is he within his rights?'

She maintained her half-embarrassed silence. I turned away in disgust. 'It's like talking to a pair of window dummies.' I slammed my way out to the hall.

Debbie was emerging from the living-room, closing the door with caution. I said, 'Is she all right?'

'Sound asleep. I gave her the maximum dose.'

Lowering my voice, I said, 'Come down here. I want to talk to you.'

After some hesitation, she followed. Inside the cloak-room, alert for the telephone bell, I spoke swiftly. 'Be truthful with me, Debbie. What's it really all about? Why were you digging in that patch?'

'I told you. For exercise.'

'You think anyone believes that?'

'I don't care if they believe it or not.'

'Don't you mind what *I* think?'

She stared at the floor. 'I used to. Then you came over different, and I didn't any more.'

My limbs clamped, as if someone had activated a central locking device. 'Different?'

'Ask Carol. She'll tell you.'

'I can't ask Carol, for God's sake. She's out cold. You explain.'

'How can I?' Debbie's head moved in a hunted way from side to side. 'You just . . . changed, that's all.'

'Most people do, from time to time. Was it in some particular respect?'

'If you don't know, I can't see how I can tell you.'

'Of course you can tell me! Was I rude to you? Unkind?'

'Oh, you've always been quite polite.'

'What kind of a remark is that?'

'No, you were never unkind. In a way, I wish you had been. At least it would have shown you were *involved*.'

'Involved with what, in heaven's name?'

Debbie's shoulders gave an agitated heave. 'Things in general. The family.'

'You mean, I've been giving the impression . . .' I thought urgently. 'When did you first notice this apparent alteration?'

'It wasn't just apparent, Dad.' She spoke earnestly, more freely, as if a logjam had been cleared. 'Honestly, you've not been the same. Carol and I, we both noticed it. You used to take an interest in what we were doing, but then suddenly . . . It wasn't our imagination. You became sort of . . . distant.'

'I've had a lot on my mind. The firm—'

'If it was business, you'd have told us about it, wouldn't you? You always did. You used to come home full of your troubles, and we'd all listen and sympathize. But then you stopped doing that.'

'When?'

'I can't put an exact date on it. Several years ago.'

I glared at the coat-rack. 'How about Pete? Did he notice?'

'I don't know. He's a bit vague, like you. It might not have struck him like it did us.'

'Did I do anything objectionable?'

'You didn't do a thing. That's the point. As far as we're concerned, you might as well not have been in the house.'

I felt a surge of resentment. 'Sure you're not exaggerating, love? Absent-minded I may be at times . . .'

Her head shook relentlessly. 'It's more than that.'

I waited vainly for enlargement. 'If I was that bad,' I said eventually, 'why didn't you let me know? I could have done something about it.'

'Mum asked us not to. She said it would only cause trouble.'

My head rocked. 'She'd noticed it too?'

'Naturally she had. When someone goes around

looking like a zombie, you can't very well shut your eyes to it.'

'Have I really been doing that?'

'It's just a figure of speech, but it's not so far off the mark. Sometimes, when you look at people . . . Do you remember a couple of weeks ago, I showed you a new dress I'd bought?'

I ransacked my memory. 'The green-striped one?'

'I had that last year,' she said crisply. 'This was creamy-white, with scarlet trimming.'

'I remember.'

'No, you don't, because that's the wrong description. You see? I knew you weren't paying any attention. You were looking in my direction and making noises, but you weren't *there*. You were somewhere else. Now do you see what I'm getting at?'

'To the average man, women's clothes—'

'I'm only giving one tiny example. There are dozens more I could mention.'

'Are you saying,' I asked slowly, 'that this attitude of mine—assuming you're right about it—could be responsible for what's happened to your mother?'

Debbie fingered a coat that hung from a nearby peg. 'We don't know what's happened to her.'

'That's no answer.'

'All right, then! Yes, I do think there's a connection. I don't know what it is and I don't know whether you do, but it's too much of a—'

The telephone shrilled. Giving her a *wait a bit* gesture, I hurried across the hall and claimed the receiver before Merton could reach it. 'Pete?'

'No. Me, I'm afraid.' The sound of Eleanor's clear voice was like a punch in the solar plexus. 'Can you talk?'

'Not at the moment.' I kept my gaze steadfastly on Merton, who was listening brazenly from the kitchen doorway. 'It'll have to wait, Eleanor. Leave it till the morning, then try to sort it out with Cliff. I may be in later.'

'Is that last bit accurate?'

'I hope so.'

'Okay, see you then. Try to make it, because there's something we have to discuss. 'Bye now.'

'Good night, Eleanor. Thank you for ringing.'

Hanging up, I looked from Merton to Debbie. 'Just my assistant flapping. She's looking after things.'

'Same as she always does.' There was a diamond edge to Debbie's voice. Merton surveyed her with interest.

'Still nothing from France?' he enquired.

'If there had been I'd have told you, if only to get rid of you.'

'Phyllis and I,' he announced, as though addressing a lifelong acquaintance at a cocktail-party, 'are about to scram for the night. We shan't be far, though. You'll remember what I said?'

'I'll try. You know what my memory is, these days.'

'Let us know about young Peter in the morning, huh? One way or the other.'

'Can't wait for our next chat,' I said sarcastically. 'O-nine-hundred, on the dot.'

With a flap of a hand he vanished. A moment later, the kitchen's outer door opened and shut.

Beckoning to Debbie, I went through and rearranged a couple of chairs so that they faced each other at an angle beside the table. All the cups and saucers had been washed and stacked neatly on the drainer. As Debbie came in, I sat on one of the chairs and indicated the other. Moving it away a little, she occupied it and sat investigating her nails. I looked reflectively at the top of her head.

'In my opinion,' I told her, 'it's high time we got down to basics.'

★

She looked up. 'What do you mean?'

'I think you know perfectly well what I mean.'

Her left hand made a nervous movement, as if it were something separate from the rest of her. 'If it's the hole in the garden . . .'

'What else?'

'I still say it's my business.'

'Don't be childish. We both know why you were digging there.'

'Why ask, then?'

'I was hoping we might thrash it out, reach an understanding. You see, Debbie, I don't blame you altogether for entertaining rather bizarre ideas. You're under a lot of stress, and I can appreciate that my behaviour . . . Tell me something. When did you first find out about Eleanor and me?'

She flushed crimson. Looking away, she said in a low voice, 'I just gradually came to realize. Small things that happened — it wasn't hard to piece them together. We compared notes, Carol and I . . .'

'Notes. That's nice.'

'You'd have done the same,' she said challengingly.

'Maybe.' I considered the situation for a while. It was all rather messier than I had imagined. At last I said, 'And your mother? Did she know?'

'I'm not sure. Truly, Dad. I can't say. There is one thing, though. You know this rheumatic complaint she had, poly . . . I can never say it.'

'Polymyalgia rheumatica.'

'Well, it came on about three years ago, right? Just about the time you started looking dreamy and forgetful.' Debbie looked at me fully for the first time. 'When was it that you and Eleanor . . . ?'

I moved uncomfortably. 'We got serious about four years back. What are you suggesting?'

'There's probably no link. Only there are some doctors

who think that poly-whatsit could stem from some hormonal imbalance brought on by stress, and it was just a year or so after you got tied up with Eleanor that Mum went down with it, so I did wonder . . .'

'My God. That's all I needed.'

'We've no proof,' she hedged. 'Mum may not even have suspected.'

'I'd have laid odds she didn't. She's always seemed placid enough, except just briefly when she was in such pain. And as far as that goes, the tablets did the trick, didn't they? Cured her in no time.'

'She's certainly kept jolly active.'

'On the other hand,' I continued after a period of reflective silence, 'if there's anything in what you say, it does throw a possible new light on the mystery. She might suddenly have decided she couldn't take it any longer — Eleanor and me, that is.'

'And just walked out?'

'Without knowing what she was up to.'

'In that case,' argued Debbie, her voice betraying distress, 'why hasn't she been found? She couldn't just melt away.'

'It's been known for people to —'

The telephone shrilled. Beating Debbie to the door, I got to the instrument first, confident that this time I was going to hear Peter's voice. This time I wasn't mistaken. His youthful baritone came through loud and clear. 'Dad? Can you hear me?'

'I can hear you, Pete, thank heavens. Are you all right? We've been frantic. The French police —'

'You needn't tell me. I've had it all from Madame Bardeau. Sorry it's taken so long, but we drove into this pine forest and . . . Tell you about it later. Any news of Mum?'

'None, old chap, I'm sorry to say. We just don't know what to make of it. She's been gone three days.'

'Just vanished?'

'Simply wandered off and didn't come back. Can you get home, Pete, as fast as possible? Sorry, but I think you should be here. First, though, I'd like your opinion on one thing. You know the photo you took of Mum?'

'The portrait study? Back at Christmas?'

'We've handed it to the police. What I want to know is, what do you think of it?'

'What do I think?' he said after a blank interval.

'What's your rating of it as a likeness?' I glanced at Debbie, who was watching me intently.

'As a matter of fact,' Peter replied, 'without wanting to brag, I thought it was spot-on. Is someone saying it's not?'

CHAPTER FOURTEEN

The office was empty when I arrived. No incoming calls had been recorded. Eleanor's shoulder-strap bag, however, lay on her desk alongside the gold-plated lighter I had given her a year previously: I guessed she had slipped out for cigarettes. Wheeling out my own chair, I slumped into it and spread out the newspapers I had bought at the corner shop.

Peter's shot of his mother had been faithfully reproduced in most of them. All had carried it on an inside page, with brief caption stories, under headings like *Wife Vanishes* or *Puzzle of the Missing Home-Lover*. The details given were basic. To date, the curiosity of Fleet Street had evidently not been excited too keenly. I had been warned not to count on a perpetuation of this.

For my part, I was still gazing at a stranger. Try as I might, I was utterly unable to see Sara in the chubby-featured, button-eyed face that confronted me from the newsprint. Idiotically, I turned from one edition to

another in a bid to find a single picture that was unlike all
the rest: the same unrecognizable image kept hitting me
as I flipped the sheets. I was just casting the whole stack
despairingly aside when Eleanor returned, holding cigarettes and a string bag of groceries which she hung on a
vacant prong of the coat-stand in passing. From the far
side of her desk she surveyed me inscrutably.

'I see you're finally in print.'

I responded with an over-elaborate shrug. 'Now we
await the newshounds, apparently. Once they get the
scent, I'm for it.'

'They're likely to chase it up?'

'The cops seem to think so. News editors feed on
riddles.'

Thoughtfully releasing a pack from its wrapper, she
extracted a cigarette and threw it on my blotter before
taking out another, striking flame from the lighter, leaning across to hold it steady for me, doing the same for
herself. Twin plumes of smoke climbed to the ceiling.
Inhaling again, she said a little throatily, 'What's special
about this one? People vanish all the time.'

'It's not every day their husbands can't describe them.'

'You'll be wishing you'd kept your mouth shut.'

'How was I to know? I just said what came automatically. I never dreamt I'd finish up in a minority of one.'

She looked contemplatively at the smoke. 'Any word
from Peter?'

'He rang last night. Be home this evening.' I met her
eyes. 'He remembers the photo. Thinks the likeness is
terrific.'

Perching on the rim of her desk, Eleanor tapped ash
over the carpet and made no comment. I glanced at the
cubicle door. 'Where's Tina?'

'Tina called,' she replied expressionlessly, 'to say she
wouldn't be in. Feels under the weather.'

I looked vacantly at the mail in my in-tray. Eleanor

said, 'I'll deal with that presently, if you like. How did you make out with the fuzz?'

'Last night? Or this morning?'

She looked questioning. Briefly relating the events of the previous evening, I added, 'Sinclair came to the house early this morning. Said he'd circulated the photo to the Press and hoped it might lead to something. Then he gave me another grilling.'

'I thought you looked browned off. Same approach?'

'Essentially. More or less accusing me of having something to hide. Hinting that they might be excavating other parts of the garden in due course. The entire damn half-acre, for all I know.'

'Think he's serious?'

'Up to a point. He can see for himself, most of it's already been planted out with shrubs or vegetables. But I guess he might argue that any of it could have been lifted temporarily, then replaced . . .' I looked dully at Eleanor through the fumes. 'It's as much as I can do to believe fifty per cent of what I'm saying.'

'You'll adjust,' she said coolly. After a moment she added, 'Why would he hint like that? Seems like inviting you to dig up Sara—if he really thinks you've buried her—and ferry her off somewhere else during the night.'

'Fat chance. They're watching me round the clock.' Meeting her eye, I gestured at the window. 'Glance out. You'll probably see an unmarked saloon parked on the yellow band with a view of the building. The moment I leave here, they'll pick up their skirts and follow.'

'My! They are taking it seriously.'

'Sinclair has this hunch. I'm the prime specimen, the guy under pressure who . . .' I paused. 'How did you get on with him last night? You said we had something to discuss.'

'We're discussing it,' she said tersely.

'I imagined it might be some other aspect. It was

Sinclair you spoke to?'

'The heavy, in person.' She surveyed me over her cigarette. 'I have to say, we got along quite well. I found him reasonably forthcoming. He asked about Our Relationship—yours and mine—and I obliged by confirming it. No point in denials, was there?'

'Not a lot.' I fingered an unopened envelope. 'Did he touch on anything else?'

'Only Tina.'

My fingers froze on the vellum paper. 'How did she come into it?'

One side of Eleanor's mouth twisted into something that wasn't a smile. 'Funny you should ask that. It came as something of a bombshell to me, too. Quite honestly, it floored me for a while.' Her mouth clicked back into place. 'But I'm on my feet again now, Ralphie. I've recaptured my senses. Also my voice.'

'Linny, I was going to tell you about Tina . . .'

'No, you weren't.' Her contempt drilled into me like bee-stings. 'You were going to keep it all nice and separate—another little romp on the side—for just as long as you could, and let the future take care of itself. Right? Don't bother to answer. I know you, my sweet, better than you know yourself. The one thing I'm asking myself is, knowing you as I do, and bearing in mind the size of this office, how the hell could I have been so deaf and blind?'

I sat in silence, digesting the revised situation. Stubbing her cigarette, Eleanor folded her arms and inspected me with a kind of weary malevolence.

'But for the guileless intervention of Inspector Sinclair,' she resumed presently, 'who obviously never dreamt I could still be in the dark about it, I suppose I'd have gone on not knowing. You've played it cagey, the pair of you, I'll give you that. Once or twice I've thought you've given her one of your looks, but I put that down to routine

Brent susceptibility. I didn't cotton on to the fact that she was . . .' Eleanor drew in a slow, deep breath. 'And here was little old me, fondly imagining that all I had to contend with was a neurotic wife. Just goes to show how the best of us can be deceived.'

Her study of me intensified. 'Fairly committed, is she? Young Tina?'

'Possibly.' There seemed no point in dissembling further.

'Not that it would worry you, to that extent. Unless of course she became an embarrassment.' Eleanor tilted her head. 'Maybe that's already the situation? She's twisting your arm more than you —'

'For Pete's sake, Eleanor. Must you keep on? Can't you appreciate the mess I'm in?'

'Oh, I can see that.' Her voice had dipped, become softer. 'I can make that out very distinctly.'

Tired of confronting her from a lesser attitude, I stood up. 'What exactly did you tell Sinclair last night?'

Accentuating the slant of her head, she considered. 'I'm not sure I *told* him very much at all. Just answered his questions, like a dutiful citizen. The Inspector struck me as someone who didn't need guidance in putting two and three together. Or am I wrong? You know him better than I do.'

'Will you stop prevaricating? It's obvious you just went along with him, never even attempted to cover up for me. What did he do — suggest that you and Tina were fighting over me and I was getting desperate? And what was your reply? Yes, Officer, that's perfectly correct. Mr Brent had to make a choice between his family and one of us, and he had to make it fast. Is this what you told him, as a dutiful citizen?'

Her face remained expressionless. 'That's not bad. In a spy thriller, it would turn out you'd been equipped with a bugging device.'

I took a turn around the office. 'By Christ, Eleanor. I never reckoned on . . .' Abruptly I came to a halt. 'Did he ask you about anything else?'

'Such as what?' she enquired demurely.

'You know damn well what I'm talking about. Office matters. Business information.'

The faintest of smiles lurked at her glossed lips. 'Assuming he may have done, my pet, you can't think I'd have gone to the length of telling him about them?' Helping herself to a selection of the envelopes in the tray, she dropped them daintily on her desk and picked up a paperknife. 'Not yet, at any rate.'

I was still shaking when I got back to the Ambassador and drove it ferociously out of the car park.

For the moment, I forgot I was being shadowed. The whole of my attention focused on the scene I had just walked away from: the sight of Eleanor's derisive face, the feel of the whiplash in her voice. Above all, I was thinking of the things I might have said, and hadn't.

Beyond question, Eleanor had gained the best of it. She had me pinned to the floor and could claim the submission when she pleased. And I was under no illusion: there could be no appeal to her better nature. She lacked one. Although I had always been dimly aware of this, until now it hadn't seemed to matter. She was fun to be with, exciting, a risky but exquisite diversion. I had chosen to ignore the warning signs that the temporary route might end in a riverbed.

Absorbed by the dilemma, I failed to register the progress of a pedestrian who was stepping on to a light-controlled crossing fifty yards ahead. Too late, signals flashed to my brain. The woman was at the centre mark when I stamped on the footbrake: by the time the car had started to squeal and slew she was making a lumbering run, far too slow, for the opposite kerb, placing herself

directly in line for catastrophe. In panic, I spun the wheel
the other way.

The car straightened violently before switching course.
Both of us were now heading for the signal-stanchion;
luckily I arrived first. The green-painted column rushed
at my windscreen and then I seemed to be at the centre of
an explosion. Somebody was talking into my right ear.

I stared uncomprehendingly into a large, lugubrious
face. 'What did you say?'

The woman I had nearly run down, a mountainous
elderly creature laden with shopping-bags, was eyeing me
resentfully from the footway and complaining to by-
standers. My right elbow sagged as the car door was
wrenched open. 'Can you move?' asked the face.

Releasing the seat-belt, I tottered into the road and was
grasped supportively. 'Want to lie down, chum? Over
there, on the—'

'I'm all right.' Shaking him off, I turned to peer
dazedly at the car which had pulled up behind mine in a
yelp of rubber. Two young men emerged, approached in
a businesslike way.

'In a hurry, Mr Brent?' The shorter of the pair surveyed
the crumpled front of the Ambassador and the realigned
stanchion, now blocking the footway like a lowered rail-
crossing barrier. 'A man in your position should really
take more care.'

'I missed her, didn't I? She stepped off too suddenly.'

'Lights were against you,' he pointed out. 'If you
wouldn't mind stepping over here . . .'

An hour later a breakdown truck arrived to tow the car
away. By that time I had given my account to a traffic
policeman, and the pedestrian had volubly had her say
and gone home to cook lunch. My knees had become
gelid. I was invited into the following car, a Rover with no
distinguishing marks and an embracing rear seat into
which I sank with a feeling of faintness that irked me.

The two young men returned to their places in front. With the show over, the onlookers began to disperse.

Detaching something from beneath the fascia, the driver's colleague spoke into it. A voice babbled something in reply. He glanced meaningfully at the driver, who fired the engine and made a cautious U-turn in the road. I said feebly, 'I'd like to get home as soon as possible. My daughters are expecting me.'

Neither of them replied. We drove fast but smoothly back the way we had come, reaching my office building at the same time as an official police car jerked to a halt outside it, disgorging three men in plain clothes and a uniformed sergeant. One of the trio was Inspector Sinclair. He lobbed a glance our way before hurrying after the others into the premises. The sergeant approached us, exchanged brief inaudible words at the window with the driver, opened the rear door and clambered inside to sit next to me. We waited in silence.

I wanted to say, 'What is this? What's going on?' The syllables refused to form. Delayed shock was doing its work: in a condition of semi-numbness, I wondered cloudily whether Peter had managed to book a flight and had arrived safely at Heathrow. I was anxious to be there to greet him when he got home. For some reason it was important to me that I should be the first to speak to him. The compulsion was ironic. I hadn't paid any particular attention to him in years.

Half an hour limped by. The two in front muttered occasionally, scraps of dialogue that I couldn't catch. I yearned to stretch my legs. Summer had revived and was basting the streets, rocketing the temperature inside the car. Alongside me, the sergeant lowered his window an inch or two, alleviating the stuffiness but not the heat. The man in front of me opened the passenger window. That made it bearable.

From the building's front entrance a figure emerged.

Approaching in his unmistakable lurching style, Sinclair opened the offside rear door and beckoned the sergeant out. Then he took his place, closed the door, wound up the window. He sat looking steadily into my face.

'Want to tell us about it, Mr Brent?'

It was like the tenth re-run of an old movie. Parched of throat, I said hoarsely, 'You're not serious? I've been answering your questions for three days. What more do you want to know?'

'You haven't answered this one. Why did you kill her?'

He gave me time. Eventually I found breath and was able to speak. 'You've found her, then? Where was she?'

'I believe you know that already.'

I stared at him apathetically. 'If I'd known where she was,' I explained with some care, mingled with indifference, 'I wouldn't have been trying so hard to find her all this time. Am I crazy, or are you?'

Something in his eyes perplexed me. After a moment he spoke again, quietly. 'I think you misunderstand me, Mr Brent. It's not your wife I'm talking about. It's your assistant, Mrs Somerville.'

CHAPTER FIFTEEN

In mid-afternoon there was a break in the interrogation and I was given half an hour to myself with a cup of tea. For lunch they had brought me fried eggs and bacon, the stench of which had turned my stomach. With the tea, I succeeded in nibbling at part of a digestive biscuit. After that I was escorted for the third time to the lavatory. On my return, Sinclair was there again, impassive.

'Had any second thoughts, Mr Brent?'

'You don't get me that way.' I adjusted my chair so as to mitigate the ache that was building up in my thigh-muscles. 'I don't intend to oblige with a false confession, for you or anybody else.'

'I don't think that's quite fair,' he said clemently. 'Have I twisted your arm? I'm simply giving you the opportunity—'

'Forget it. I'd nothing to do with her death, and that's final.'

He allowed one of his celebrated pauses. 'You were heard to be quarrelling.'

'By a switchboard girl. Fifteen yards along the corridor. How could she know what was happening?'

'She couldn't. Not in detail. I've seen for myself how the first floor is partitioned: anything she heard must have been garbled—I accept that. But you do admit that you and Mrs Somerville were having words?'

'A lively exchange, I'd call it. Yes, there was a point at issue which I may have got heated about. That's nothing uncommon.'

'For you it is . . . according to the switchboard girl. She'd never heard you shouting before.'

'I deny shouting.'

'She heard raised voices,' he amended graciously. 'Then your office door was flung open and you said, *Don't you threaten me, Eleanor.* You deny saying that?'

'I may have blurted something of the kind. What of it?'

'The door shut again. Then the switchboard girl heard a thump.'

'I've explained. I walked back into the coat-stand and sent it flying. After I'd picked it up—'

'A minute or two later, Doris Ward heard the door reopen and footsteps going quickly away downstairs. Your typist has been off sick today, right? So it could only have been you.'

'I'm not disputing it,' I said. 'I did hurry off. I was anxious to get home.'

'Mrs Somerville was alive and well when you left?'

'No. She was flat out across her desk, bleeding to death.'

The peculiar look returned to his eyes. 'Possibly you're not aware, Mr Brent, that what you've just given me is an almost exact description of how she was found?'

The ceiling fell on me. From amid the wreckage I said shakily, 'It was only surmise. When I last saw her she was sitting on the desk, opening the mail, so naturally . . . Who did find her?'

'Doris, the switchboard girl.' Sinclair seemed to hesitate, before reaching a decision to continue. 'After hearing the footsteps going away, she tells us, she was kept busy with calls for twenty minutes until her relief arrived to let her take a coffee break. As she was passing your office door, Doris says she felt suddenly uneasy. It seemed very quiet. She knocked, got no answer, so she opened the door and looked inside. That's when she saw Mrs Somerville. Her body was lying across the desk, as you've just said. Doris immediately called the police.'

He engineered a pause of more than standard weight and duration. 'Why did you kill your assistant?'

I sat staring down at the table. Part of my mind, absurdly, was preoccupied with the question of how many other suspects had suffered here before me, fumbling to compose phrases of rebuttal that would carry the ringing note of conviction. It was a losing battle. In defence, there was no security. I decided on attack.

'What weapon was used?'

Sinclair said nothing.

'I've a right to be told,' I said sharply. 'Was she stabbed? Strangled?'

A shadow of uncertainty passed across his eyes. 'Why don't you try remembering?'

'I do remember. Perfectly. I picked up the coat-stand, said a few more words to Eleanor—*Hold the fort, I'm off home:* something on those lines—and left her slitting envelopes with a paperknife. Then I . . .' A thought clouted me. 'She was stabbed with the paperknife? Is that it?'

Sinclair said non-committally. 'It's starting to come back?'

'It never went, damn you. My own actions are clear in my mind. You needn't try smudging them with mythical ones. It won't work.'

He seemed grudgingly impressed. Having given the matter some more thought, he said slowly, 'I'm going right out on a limb. I'll tell you the cause of death, Mr Brent. Mrs Somerville was struck on the back of the head with the glass paperweight from your desk. Does that signify anything to you?'

'*Signify?* That thing weighs three pounds, if it weighs an ounce. Did it . . . ?'

'She was probably killed outright,' he said brusquely.

I made helpless gestures with both hands. 'What can I say? It wasn't me. I could never . . . Fingerprints? Mine are on it, presumably. Anyone else's?'

'We're checking.'

'It wasn't me,' I reiterated.

'Be fair.' Fatigue was starting to seep into his voice. 'You and she were heard arguing. At around ten-forty you were seen leaving the building, clearly in a bit of a state. At eleven, Doris Ward opened your office door and discovered the body. How does that tot up, to you?'

'Try a spot of fairness yourself,' I retorted. 'Soon after nine this morning you were round at my house, asking yet more questions. When I left to drive to Wimbledon, I knew I was being tailed. Aware of this, I then proceeded to attack and kill my assistant—in full view, so to speak? You must think I'm out of my mind.'

'Maybe that's what you intended us to assume.'

'I don't have to listen to rubbish like this.'

'Your love-life,' he said remorselessly, 'was in a

thoroughgoing tangle, wasn't it? Shall I tell you what I think? Mrs Somerville was turning the screw, so you lashed back. A singleminded lady, your assistant — I gathered that much when I talked to her last night. Fairly persistent, I fancy, when she chose to be. Becoming something more than an embarrassment, was she, Mr Brent?'

Although I heard what he was saying, I found it relatively easy to disregard. My brain was racing on other tracks. Waiting until he stopped, I said estimatingly, 'After hearing us argue, Doris Ward was occupied with calls on her switchboard — right?'

He nodded briefly, knocked out of his stride.

'So, in the course of that twenty minutes, what was to prevent someone else from slipping into my office, unseen and unheard, to kill Eleanor?'

'Why in hell should they?'

'Maybe she had enemies. She was the type of person who might.'

'You're probably the best judge of that.' He contemplated me thoughtfully. 'Can you suggest anyone?'

'I employ three drivers, for a start.' I thought feverishly. 'I've lost track of their movements for the past three days. Eleanor was handling all that for me. But you could try questioning them. Then there's my solicitor, Clifford English. He and Eleanor saw a good deal of each other. They could have fallen out.'

'Scratching around a little, aren't we?' Nevertheless he was scrawling notes on a jotter.

'A cornered animal,' I reminded him, 'does tend to use its claws. In my position, wouldn't you be doing the same?'

Two hours later I was again taken back to the interrogation room. Sinclair, wearing a tired, tight frown, came in with a short and rotund man who looked as if he had strayed from a Buster Keaton silent comedy and was trying to grope his way back. He examined me in a deadpan manner as he bounced into a chair on the far side of the table. Seating himself gingerly to my right, the Inspector brooded for a spell.

He said abruptly, 'There's been a development.'

I waited.

Indicating his companion, Sinclair added, 'This is Chief Superintendent Burns, who's in charge of the murder enquiry. He's got something to ask you.'

I transferred my attention. Burns made some quick, nodding movements, like a sparrow pecking. His voice was startlingly *profundo*.

'Just a simple query, Mr Brent. When did you first tell your typist, Christina Harwood, about your relationship with Mrs Somerville?'

Alert for traps, I sat gazing at him. 'I didn't,' I said finally. 'She had no idea.'

'You sound very positive.'

'I've reason to be. What does this—'

'Tell me about your reasons.'

In an effort to concentrate, I closed my eyes. 'A couple of days ago, Tina and I had a talk. She did drop a remark on the way Mrs Somerville looked at me sometimes, but from her other comments it was obvious she had no suspicion of anything between us. Then, in a . . . later discussion, she was agitated about my wife. It was her she saw as an obstacle, not Mrs Somerville.'

Reopening my eyes, I caught Burns sliding a glance at the Inspector and giving a slight nod. 'Thank you.' He stood up.

'Just a moment.' I matched his action. 'What's this about? I feel I've a right to know.'

'You'll hear,' he said briefly, and oscillated from the room.

Sinclair lingered. 'Last night,' he informed me, 'I interviewed Miss Harwood at her home.'

'Somehow I guessed you might. And you told her about Mrs Somerville and me?'

'I clarified the situation.'

'What effect did it seem to have on her?'

With a slight shrug, he left the room.

I was talking to Clifford English when the cell door opened and the duty officer reappeared. 'Sorry to interrupt,' he said, 'but I don't think you'll be needing your lawyer so urgently, Mr Brent, after all. If both you gentlemen would care to step this way . . .'

Sinclair spoke to us in a small, bare room opposite the duty sergeant's counter. 'Officially I can't comment at this stage, but off the record, Mr English, in view of what your client has been through, I'm making an exception.' He glanced at me. 'Perhaps you won't be surprised to learn that Christina Harwood has confessed to the murder of Mrs Somerville.'

The confirmation was anti-climax. English's fingers gripped my arm: it was only then that I realized I was swaying. Planting my feet wider, I leaned back against the wall, took a few deep breaths.

'You've definite proof?' I heard him ask.

'A silver crucifix of hers. It was found under Mrs Somerville's desk, with blood on it. Must have come off as she aimed the blows. Blood's not been analysed yet, but it's a cinch it'll belong to the dead woman's group.'

'Has the crucifix been positively identified?' demanded English.

'Yes, by Miss Harwood's parents. Anyway, it's academic. The girl's admitted all that's necessary.'

'Briefly . . . can you say how she did it?'

'Told her parents she felt poorly and wanted to sleep. Then she slipped on a dark wig—one of several she has—and a pair of glasses, left the house without her mother knowing and walked to the office, ten minutes away. By chance, she must have got there just after Mr Brent had gone. Nobody saw her arrive or leave.'

English gave me an anxious glance. 'She was able to take Mrs Somerville unawares?'

'Seems the victim was sitting on the desk with her back to the door, dictating a letter into the audio. Miss Harwood went in softly, picked up the paperweight from the other desk . . .' Sinclair gesticulated graphically. 'She's a well-built girl, pretty strong. And half-demented at the time. Mrs Somerville quite frankly never stood a chance.'

'I see.' English puffed out his cheeks, looking for the moment like an overfed schoolboy. 'Thank you, Inspector. In all the circumstances, we appreciate your candour. In turn, I'm sure you appreciate that my client is feeling more than a little threadbare right now. All right for us to be off?'

'Provided Mr Brent goes straight home. We'll want to be in touch with him.'

'Of course. I'll take him there myself. Ready, Ralph? I've got the car outside.'

During the homeward journey I came out of coma long enough to say, 'Can we have them for wrongful arrest?'

English shook his head over the wheel. 'They'd plenty of justification for questioning you and they were only doing their job.' Changing gear, he threw me a quick look. 'There's still a sticky time ahead, Ralph — you realize that? Court hearings, bad publicity. You've got to be prepared . . .'

'Thanks for the caution.' I sat staring ahead. Presently I added, 'I wonder how Tina's feeling.'

CHAPTER SIXTEEN

Both girls emerged from the kitchen to greet us. Debbie, slightly breathless, said, 'There's a meal ready, if you want it. Will you be staying, Mr English?'

'Thanks, no. I must cut along. I'll leave you to look after your father. He's had rather a rough time.'

Debbie looked at me with an indefinable expression. 'Is he in the clear?'

'Absolutely, I'm relieved to say. I'm afraid I can't stop to explain all the detail. He'll tell you about it.'

Carol said, 'We're not really interested in the details.'

English regarded her uncertainly. A tallish, gawky man of fifty, head of a family which tallied to a nicety with the national average, he harboured an acute sense of the proprieties. Notwithstanding his professional detachment, his personal feelings had plainly taken a hammering already. Coming partly to life, I ducked into the conversation.

'You'll have to bear with us, Cliff, for a while. It's all been a shade traumatic.' With a sign to the girls, I steered him back along the hall to the street door. 'Sure you won't stay? Well, thanks for everything. See you tomorrow, as arranged. No, I won't answer any more questions unless you're there. Yes, I'll consider a full statement . . .'

From the porch, I watched him return to his Audi and accelerate off, a stiff-backed, tense-lipped figure at the wheel. As I turned to go indoors, somebody waved to me from the other side of the street: Arthur Bowers, trudging home from the station after a day's toil at the Civic Centre. In eleven years we had exchanged perhaps a dozen words, but invariably we waved. Mechanically conforming to custom, I flapped a hand, closed the door. All over the place, people were walking home from the station. Striding indoors, to be greeted by wives, children, dogs. The TV tuned to the early evening news. *Anything worth watching later? There's this thriller about a man whose wife goes missing* . . .

Carol had remained standing in the hall, awaiting my re-entry. In a thin sweater and baggy jeans, she looked more than ever the huge-eyed, famished waif. Putting out a hand, I said, 'Bearing up, love? I'm sorry about all this.'

Evading the hand, she beckoned me into the living-room. With a feeling of tense apprehension I followed her, convinced that I should find the Rev. Lionel Gooch in sanctimonious occupation of the sofa, primed to deliver a Godly broadside. The room, however, was empty. Taking up a stance with her back to a radiator, Carol submitted the pattern of the carpet to a closer investigation than it seemed to warrant, and said nothing.

I considered narrowing the physical gap between us. Then I thought again, and stayed where I was. There were, I suspected, a great many things I craved to say to my younger daughter. I couldn't fasten on one of them.

Suddenly, still looking at the carpet, she spoke. 'Peter phoned. The flight was delayed, so he won't be home till later.'

'Oh. What time?'

'It's a bit uncertain. Some industrial trouble with ground staff. He'll call again from Heathrow.'

'When he does, I'll go and pick him up.' Then I remembered. 'Hell, I've smashed my car. I'll have to take the Metro.'

'It's not being used.' Her face came up and I saw her features crumple; diving forward, I caught the first explosion of tears on my shirt-front. This time she didn't try to dodge. Locked quiveringly together, we stayed there for a couple of minutes while she regained control

of herself and I gazed out at the garden, which already
was acquiring a fine coating of neglect, like summer
mould on a loaf. I tried to recall a time when things had
been commonplace. Just now, any such condition seemed
insanely out of reach.

The door opened to admit Debbie and a whiff of
bacon-fat. Sizing up the situation, she came directly
across and put her arms around both of us. Carol sniffed
a few times. Addressing Debbie over her right shoulder, I
said thickly, 'This is all getting a bit emotional, I'm
afraid.'

'Don't let it scare you, Dad.'

Ushering us to the sofa, Debbie sat between us and
helped her sister mop up. My feelings wavered between
euphoria and humiliation. In a sense, it was the way I
should have felt if, at the height of a business crisis, the
office cleaner had thrown a glance at the main ledger,
planted a chapped finger against an entry and announced, 'There's yer trouble.' Grateful as I was for an
uplift, I couldn't help wishing it had come from another
source. In the midst of wiping Carol's cheeks, Debbie
turned her head and met my eye.

There were questions I wanted to ask her. Now, if ever,
was the moment for confidences, the bartering of inner
thoughts: the chance might never recur. Gathering
breath, I leaned forward to give utterance. As I did so,
the telephone rang.

'That'll be Pete.' Astonishingly, my voice sounded
normal. I rose from the cushions. 'You two stay here. I'll
get it.'

After picking up the receiver, I held it for a moment
while I assembled a few remaining fragments of com-
posure. 'Pete?' I said, shakily but with passable aplomb.
'Are you calling from the airport?'

My ear picked up a confusion of sounds, terminating in
a rattle. After a period of total silence a voice came on as

though at a given signal, clear and assured, female, touched with what might have been asperity. 'Mr Brent?'

'Speaking.' My mind was still at Heathrow. Terror bit into me. 'What is it? Has there been a crash?'

The voice ignored the query. 'I'm calling on behalf of your wife. At least I think I am. We've a lady here who looks very much like the picture in today's *Telegraph*. Would you like to come along and see her?'

After the stately power of the Ambassador, the more kittenish antics of the Metro took some getting used to. From the rear seat, Debbie said tautly, 'Easy, Dad. You've had your accident for today. Let's get there in one piece.'

Throttling back, I did my best to heed her advice through the rest of the suburban area, picking up speed again as we reached a stretch of open road. Next to me, I could feel the tension of Carol's body. Spotting a sign to Epsom, I veered left at a fork and immediately was forced to slacken off behind a heavy goods vehicle whose driver was being paid for time in the cab and was behind with his mortgage. Hugging its tailboard, I said breathlessly, 'I only hope Pete gets the message when he lands. If not, he'll wonder where the heck we are.'

'Usually they're pretty good,' Debbie said confidently, 'with the P.A. announcements. Anyway, Inspector Sinclair said he'd send someone to keep an eye on the house, didn't he? They'd catch Pete if he arrived.'

'Get a move on, Dad,' breathed Carol. 'Can't you get past?'

Taking a risk, I left the lorry behind on a curve and worked the needle to fifty-five. The legal limit was forty. Although Debbie refrained from comment, electricity crackled between us. My driving was, I knew, almost criminally reckless, but I couldn't help myself. Beyond Epsom I took the Guildford road at a gallop, impeded here and there by remnants of the peak-hour traffic tangle, but largely able to exploit the Metro's willingness to please. When we were past Leatherhead, a hand slid across my left shoulder from the rear.

'Have a sandwich,' ordered Debbie. 'You'll collapse if you don't eat.'

Again, it was sound advice. My appetite was non-existent, but I made myself gnaw at the cheddar-filled slices while covering the distance to the Guildford by-pass. With the city behind us and unrestricted road ahead, Carol stirred as a sign displayed itself briefly to the left. 'Fourteen miles.' I nodded to indicate that I had seen, and flashed her something intended as a grin. I could see her fingers twisting nervously in her lap.

On the final ascent to Hindhead, a very large, very venerable coach transporting a number of very small, very elderly passengers loomed in front of us and stayed there at trotting pace. The curves and double centre lines precluded overtaking. There was nothing for it but to hang on to its skirts, like a disciple. Logic ruled that there was no alternative, and since logic had been in short supply for half a week I almost welcomed the need to accept it, even though part of me wanted to scream at every puff of discoloured exhaust that came from the vehicle's shuddering tailpipe. What could an extra few minutes possibly matter?

The pace of the coach dropped to a walk. Spouts of black smoke signalled a gear-change. Coming virtually to a halt, the monolith bucked, trembled, resumed the climb at a hobble. Above the level of the rearmost seat, five permed heads of grey hair remained fixed and immovable, like frostbitten cauliflowers.

Beside me, Carol squirmed in her seat, chewed at a knuckle. Maintaining a measured distance from the coach's tail-end, I leaned back in an elaborate pantomime of relaxation.

'What's the betting,' I remarked, 'they're on their way to a disco?'

A low chuckle came from behind. After a moment, Carol's shoulders jerked and a half-strangled noise escaped her. Debbie laughed outright. Carol followed suit and I joined in, a shade hysterically, until the three of us were braying like donkeys. The mood lasted us to the top of the rise, where the coach laboured back into its full twenty-miles-an-hour stride and I allowed it to pull ahead as the outskirts of the town came into sight. As quickly as it had formed, the mirth evaporated. In an uneasy silence we puttered into the town centre and turned right, as directed, at the traffic lights. Debbie leaned forward.

'Downhill,' she volunteered needlessly, 'for half a mile. Then sharp left into a driveway. Vista Cottage. It might be signed . . .'

She was right. The name showed up in scarlet lettering on a white board attached to the trunk of a beech at the driveway entrance; beneath it, a smaller sign announced VACANCIES. Steering through, I braked on a gravelled expanse alongside a Range Rover with its nose in a rhododendron.

Vista Cottage looked more the size of a small manor house. There were large amounts of weathered beam and ornamental deep red brickwork, plus a spectacular view across country. Leaving the car, the three of us stood gazing at the plant-infested front entrance with a sudden shared sense of reluctance to go further.

Debbie was first to move. 'Come on,' she said, advancing across the gravel. 'We've got to know.'

Inside, the hall of the cottage had been fashioned into a reception area with a grained-wood counter across one corner, bearing a couple of telephones, a map-rack, and piles of guide leaflets. A pegboard of keys hung on the wall behind. Treading through thick gold carpet to the counter, Debbie gave a couple of shakes to a small brass handbell, arousing echoes.

My discomfort increased. The expedition was an absurdity. Sara couldn't be here. Hindhead? We had no links with the place, recent or past. To the best of my knowledge, it meant nothing to either of us. I wanted to turn and walk out, avoid seeing anyone. As if sensing the impulse, Debbie clutched my elbow.

'Someone's coming.'

From a stairhead at the end of the hall emerged a woman of about Sara's age, beanpole-thin, clad like a lab assistant in a dark blue smock. The impression was sustained by the clinical appraisal she spread over us. I heard myself speaking huskily. 'Mrs Smithfield? We spoke on the—'

'You'll be Mr Brent.' She spoke with the clear directness of the professional analyst, giving each of the girls a brief, paralysing examination before discarding them. 'You can't have wasted much time. First of all, will you be wanting rooms for the night?'

For a moment I gaped at her. 'No,' I said, recovering, 'that won't be necessary. If the lady you have staying here is my wife, we'll want to take her back to London right away. Has she—'

'I don't think the name Brent means a thing to her.' Mrs Smithfield tested with a forefinger the dust-layer on a neglected corner of the counter, frowned, made a note on a pad suspended from her waist. 'We've talked about it and she doesn't appear to remember much at all. Except that she has an idea she might come from somewhere near London. Certainly, the Press photograph . . . When I saw the newspapers, I felt I should contact you.'

'We're most grateful. Is she around, just now?'

'Upstairs. In her room. Getting ready for dinner.' On the third particle of information Mrs Smithfield pivoted, led the way with a gesture. We clumped after her. Carol's face had set rigid. Debbie's looked impenetrable, as it always had at moments of high drama.

Mounting the stairs, I asked quietly, 'When did she arrive here?'

Mrs Smithfield halted and turned. 'Monday. Around noon.'

'Did she bring anything with her?'

'Just a small handcase. She told me she was in the neighbourhood to look up old friends, and wanted somewhere to stay for a night or two.'

'What name did she give?'

'She booked in as Mrs Baker, from Portsmouth.'

'Does she have any money?'

The manageress of Vista Cottage gave me a piercing look. 'I haven't enquired,' she said glacially. 'She paid me in cash for two nights' accommodation in advance. Beyond that . . .'

'It's not important. Has she been out much?'

'Most of the time, actually. She left quite early this morning, before the papers arrived. So it wasn't until she got back, soon after four, that I was able to check her appearance properly against the photograph and put some questions to her. It was then,' said Mrs Smithfield, showing signs of pleasure with herself, 'that she admitted having given me the first name and address that occurred to her, and that she had a memory-block.'

'She's now seen the newspaper stories, of course?'

'Oh, indeed. But none of them seem to —'

Debbie spoke up with sudden impatience. 'Does she take tablets at mealtimes?'

Mrs Smithfield contrived to ignore her while nodding in my direction. 'Breakfast and dinner. She keeps a small bottle of brown pills in her bag.' Resuming the climb, she added over a shoulder, 'Does your wife take anything like that?'

'I believe so.' I gave Debbie's hand a rallying squeeze. We had reached an elongated, creaking, artificially-lit landing and, stooped to avoid the overhanging beams, were heading for a door at the far end. The carpeting was moss-green and spongy. My heart had set up its hammering. Halting at the door, Mrs Smithfield rapped its upper panel with a set of bony knuckles and lifted her voice.

'May we come in?'

There was no reply, but almost immediately the door was opened from within and pulled back, exposing a wardrobe and part of a bedstead. Sailing through, Mrs Smithfield said on an unexpected note of kindness, 'Here we are, my dear. I've brought some visitors. Let's see whether you recognize them, shall we?'

I stepped into the bedroom.

The manageress turned expectantly to me. 'Well?' she demanded. 'Is it your wife?'

CHAPTER SEVENTEEN

In one sense, it seems a long time ago that all this occurred. Six months. Half a year.

Since then, Sara's memory seems to have performed a remarkable job of self-repair. She still has moments of vacancy, but according to the specialist this is normal and will almost certainly fade completely after a while. If not, there is little to be concerned about. 'What's a space or two, here and there?' he asks breezily. 'Less clutter for the poor old brainbox.'

Maybe he's right. Few of us can recall everything, and fewer still would care to.

Peter is back in France for Christmas. His friendship with Françoise having ripened, he now talks of gaining entry to a French provincial university, early marriage, a career in computer technology . . . Confused though his ideas seem to me, Sara remains placid enough. 'Let him get it out of his system,' she says, with a calm indulgence and a tone of finality that I find it difficult to challenge. If it were one of the girls . . . One can but speculate.

The girls? They show every sign, happily, of having regained an even keel. For a short while, Carol was inclined to be twitchy and insecure: having sailed with aplomb through her O-levels, however, she recaptured some self-confidence. To my private relief, we hear little these days about the Rev. Lionel Gooch. With an eye upon a career in biochemistry, Carol is now slogging hard for her A-levels and has small time for distraction.

Debbie, for her part, has become chief assistant to Mrs Bagshott at the Public Library and seems to be aiming for the top. The playwriting project with her friends has lurched, we gather, to a standstill. 'We've lost incentive,' is all she will say. A boy-friend, we also infer, is hovering. He too works at the Library, is constructing a treatise on middle-class reading habits, and plays chess at county standard. We are menaced with meeting him some time.

As for Sara herself . . .

It's not an easy thing to write about.

A change of footing in a relationship can be tricky enough in itself, without the added complications of a revolutionized lifestyle affecting both parties. At surface level, each of us has adapted sensibly. While unable, of course, to speak for Sara, I can say on my own behalf that, beneath it all, a great deal of bruising and a number of stress fractures have yet to heal.

As Clifford English had warned me, the period after Sara's reappearance was a sticky one. Among the worst things was Tina's trial. The hours I spent in the witness-box were not edifying, especially with the numbed eyes of her parents fixed upon me; and although I did my best to account for and justify the ultimate explosion in Tina's mind while taking care that there should be no trace of misunderstanding as to my own non-involvement in the crime itself, I emerged feeling soiled, debased, unable for a while to meet the gazes of others. It was this, as well as economic factors, that prompted a move from the district. It wasn't pleasant, either for myself or for Sara and the girls, to remain in a locality where, fairly or otherwise, I was known as the man indirectly responsible for the violent death of a woman and the indefinite detainment in a secure hospital of a girl barely out of her teens. And so our transference to a smaller property six miles distant, where we were unknown but from where Debbie could commute easily to and from the Library while Carol was able to pursue her studies at a nearby college of further education, would have been more or less inevitable regardless of the change in my own working circumstances.

Initially, I had hoped to be able to sell off the haulage business as a going concern. It speedily became plain to me, however, and was confirmed by Clifford English, that there was really nothing to offer a prospective buyer apart from the name, and this, as he observed drily, was hardly calculated at the time to pull in the customers. With the loss of Eleanor and her expertise the firm had become virtually an abstraction, and in the end I was forced to put what remained of it into liquidation and cast around for another job.

Which, at my age, was no easy matter. I had few if any specialist qualifications. During a time of recession nobody was interested, except in getting me as quickly as possible out of the door. It was a disheartening, almost panicky time, not alleviated by the fact that, after paying off the mortgage on the house we had sold, and buying the smaller one, I was left with no capital to provide a cushion. It was Sara who marched to the rescue.

In the first place, she revealed that she had more than two thousand pounds in National Savings certificates, hoarded from the housekeeping and her dressmaking earnings. This tided us over, and then, after I had finally secured what I could not help but regard as an inferior post as a sales assistant in a local do-it-yourself store, she took a quantum leap further by stepping into the position of supervisor in the design room of a clothing manufacturer with headquarters half a mile from our new address, at a salary which made mine look like pocket money out of the till.

I tried to be pleased for her. The job was a challenge which she accepted with enthusiasm and in which she soon became immersed. Now, she appears to have shed all zest for gardening and more than overcome any lingering reluctance to get out and meet people. To me, in fact, she seems fully as much of a changed person as I had taken her for, with such confusing results, in the controversial photograph.

I still think about that quite often. Try as I might, I find it impossible to dismiss from my mind the occasion of our reunion at Hindhead when, at first glance, I failed even then to recognize her immediately. But for the presence of the girls, who greeted her unhesitatingly with tears and laughter and all the other trappings of overwhelming joy and relief, I should have been at grave risk of identifying myself as the idiot of the century, or as the carrier of a new disease: matrimonial myopia. The manageress of Vista Cottage, Mrs Smithfield, is in fact probably convinced that I am one of those things, or even both. She has kept up a correspondence with Sara on a regular basis ever since, rather as though she feels that an outside check on the domestic situation is called for.

All of which is a little unfair, because Dr Ellis has explained things to me very thoroughly. It appears that the drug, a cortisone derivative, used in the treatment of *polymyalgia rheumatica*, when taken in sizeable dosages can have an inflating effect upon the flesh, creating in some instances a radical re-shaping of the original features. Sara constitutes an example. When her complaint was diagnosed, she was placed initially on a daily regimen of fifteen milligrams of Prednisolone, reduced fairly speedily to twelve and a half, then ten; at which level she remained for some months while the sedimentation count in her bloodstream came to heel. At this point, the doctor prescribed a reduction to seven and a half milligrams per day, with the hope of further retrenchment to follow.

However, he had reckoned without his patient. Always an active, vigorous person, Sara — although she hid it well — had evidently bitterly resented falling prey to such a handicapping complaint at so early an age. 'The creeping twinges,' she called it, in reference to its habit of making itself felt in different parts of the body from day to day. Finding that Prednisolone in sufficient quantity caused so dramatic an improvement, to the extent of eliminating the pains entirely, she begrudged any modification of the treatment that threatened to interfere with the process.

Basically, I understand, it was humiliation that she felt. Still in her early forties, she considered herself entitled to remain as lissom and unconstrained as she had always been; fit to tackle the housework, dressmaking, gardening; able to keep up. With an active husband several years her junior, she was determined to make no concession to human frailty. And so, for months longer than Dr Ellis was aware, she kept to a dosage of fifteen milligrams per day.

'I'm afraid,' he told me in the course of a private interview, 'I was deceived by your wife's expressed anxiety to cut down. She gulled me into believing that she was very much of an anti-tablets persuasion, whereas in fact . . .'

'You over-prescribed,' I said.

His reply was measured. 'By no means. Not at all. Once

her condition had stabilized, your wife stopped consulting me in person. Now and then, she simply left a request for more supplies of the drug with my receptionist, and I wrote out a prescription which she later collected. I thought she was down to seven and a half milligrams per day. Actually she was taking twice that.'

'When did you find out?'

'The day she came to see me about a poisoned thumb. From her facial distension, it was pretty obvious to me that she'd not been keeping to the prescribed dosage. I tackled her about it, warned her of the possible side-effects from over-medication, and she agreed to co-operate. Thereafter she did obey instructions. I kept a strict check on her supply, and she's now down to a daily maintenance dosage of four milligrams, which gives her a tolerable level of relief virtually clear of side-effects.'

'As far as her face is concerned, though, the damage was done?'

He gesticulated. 'Over-medication of that sort for a year or more . . . I expect you wondered yourself about her appearance.'

I coughed. 'Well, you know how it is. When you're living with someone and the change is gradual . . .'

How could I even hint at the truth? From the time that Sara began taking Prednisolone I was no longer with her. I was preoccupied — obsessed — by my entanglement with Eleanor; and then, in the last few months, with Tina into the bargain. In my mind's eye I was seeing only their faces. Engrossed in my juggling act, enjoying the fruits of my effortless attraction for the opposite sex, I had no attention to spare for those nearest to me. During all this time, for reasons both valid and convenient, I was putting in long hours at the office, building up the business. Such periods as I spent at home were in the nature of mere respites, hazy interludes between one bout of reality and the next. For three years or more, as I later tried to explain to Inspector Sinclair, I had barely made visual contact with my family. They had been there, around me; their talk had half-penetrated my consciousness. I hadn't seen them.

He looked at me sceptically. 'Three years?'

'You find that incredible? Just think about it. When you've been living a long time with a person, don't you come to take their presence completely for granted? You must find that. You know they're always going to be there, so you don't bother to look. Or, if you look, you don't focus. Haven't you ever eaten an entire meal with your wife without registering her?'

'Only if she's overspent at the Sales.' He gave it some thought, and a frown developed. 'You may have a point. She's always accusing me of not noticing what she's wearing . . . which quite often I don't. Anyone else, I'd automatically be cataloguing the outfit. Odd, isn't it?'

'Not really.' I warmed to my theme. 'Other people are different. Subconsciously you know their presence is temporary, so you sit up and pay attention. With familiar, established figures you can afford not to take the trouble. Half the time, therefore, you don't.'

'Half the time, maybe, but—'

'In my own case,' I intervened delicately, 'there was this extra dimension of my, um, extreme emotional involvement elsewhere. To be fair to myself,' I added, noting his expression, 'Sara did rather ask for it. I wasn't seeing such a lot of her anyway. If she wasn't dressmaking she was hoeing the garden, or else fooling around with recipes over the cooker. The fault wasn't all on one side.'

Sinclair mused briefly. 'Has it occurred to you,' he asked, 'that the reason she took up these pursuits with such abandon might have been your neglect in the first place?'

I snorted. 'If she thought I was neglecting her, why didn't she give me a punch in the mouth?'

True to his nature, he made no comment. 'What it boils down to, then,' he said presently, 'is that when you were shown a photo of your wife as she was six months ago, it didn't tally with how she looked when you last noticed her, two or three years previously?

'You say that as if you still can't believe it.'

'I'm trying.' He cogitated further. 'Why,' he murmured, 'would you want to deliberately sow confusion? You were the guy it rebounded on.'

'I'm glad you allow that.'

'One point bugs me, though,' he added. 'When the controversy over the snapshot first arose, why didn't the explanation strike either of your daughters? They knew their mother's face had altered, didn't they?'

'Of course they did. So did the neighbours. And naturally they all assumed I'd noticed it too. It happened gradually: they'd adjusted. It simply never occurred to any of them that I was still way back, three years behind, so to speak. Why should it?'

Sinclair's mouth opened, remained ajar for a moment, shut again. A kind of scowling abstraction had seized his features. He gave the impression that an entirely new set of values had suddenly been hurled at him and he was having to sift through them, sort them out. I could sympathize. I was still having a similar problem myself.

Eventually he did speak. 'Quite apart from all that,' he said slowly, 'I have to say that I agree with you, in fact, on the basic issue. Now that I've seen her in the flesh, and allowing for the effects of the drug which may have altered her face additionally in the past six months, I think it's a lousy photograph of your wife.'

'Me too,' I said fervently. 'But don't, for heaven's sake, tell my son Peter. I think he fancies himself a little at camerawork, and I'd hate to hurt his feelings.'

Sinclair leaned back reflectively. 'Dr Ellis was of the same opinion, I believe, when we showed him the snap during the investigation. But then, of course, he'd not set eyes on your wife for quite a while—not since she came to him with a septic thumb—and I suppose he reasoned that the drug must have distorted her features a bit more since that visit.'

'Which is probably right.'

'I suppose so,' he repeated. He sounded dubious. Picking up a slender ballpoint pen, he arched it between his finger and thumb until, not to my surprise, it snapped explosively and vanished into the carpet. He seemed scarcely to notice the occurrence. 'How about the mystery phone-caller?' he asked suddenly. 'And the shoulder-bag you found in the garden?'

Half a year later, my thirst for a satisfactory answer to these and other questions remains unslaked.

Various explanations have been mooted. Hotly denying that she ever made the call—in view of her loss of memory she can hardly be positive, although admittedly the voice almost certainly was not hers—Sara suggests that it could have been either Tina or Eleanor, or else a friend recruited for the purpose . . . whatever the purpose was. To flummox me, she surmises. A superfluous refinement, in my view. I was frantic from the start. But then, as she points out with a touch of acid, an outsider might not have been sure of that.

She has a point there. To others, my consternation at Sara's disappearance may have been puzzling, bearing in mind my activities in other directions. It has to be remembered, however, that there is nothing like losing a familiar object to induce grief and contrition for one's carelessness. Losing sight of a supportive domestic background is not the same thing as repudiating it. People tend to talk too glibly about such things.

As for the shoulder-bag, its origins remain a riddle. One theory is that it could have formed part of the proceeds of a burglary or mugging (crime of this type, as Sinclair himself had remarked, had been on the upsurge in the district) and was flung into our garden by the thief as he made his getaway, having removed the cash. Another is that it could have been found and carried in by a fox, which might account for the movement that Debbie thought she saw. Or else dropped by a large bird. Feasible solutions, all of them, and yet . . .

At one level, it really doesn't matter. What counts, I suppose, is that I'm a family man again, with all the built-in controls and restraints, the healthy checks and balances that the term implies. Nothing has been said, nor even insinuated. No overt pressure has been applied. There is merely a tacit acceptance of the new situation, an unspoken assumption that my deviation from the path of virtue is a thing of the past. For someone of my nature, perhaps, the discipline is needed. This is what I remind myself of, at bad moments.

Because stress, as I mentioned before, there unquestionably is. Much of it stemming, of course, from recent traumatic experiences. The residue can be attributed to role-reversal. Six months ago, I was my own boss and supported the family. Now, I am the merest cog in a miserly machine, and to a great extent my wife is the breadwinner. Self-respect can wither overnight. While not begrudging Sara her success, I have to admit that it would be easier to take if my own relative failure were less pronounced. Furthermore, it would not be unhelpful if she had remained the attentive, submissive, unobtrusive wife that she was before.

As it is, she gives the impression sometimes of living, beyond the home, an expanding life of which I can no longer hope to be a part. Truly the roles have switched. Realizing now what Sara must have endured for years, I do try to rally myself, to be a companion to her at home; but without that touch of assurance which everyone needs, the obstacles are formidable. Until now, I had no idea I could be a jealous man.

And yet I cannot bring myself to quiz her in any way. I shrink from the task, just as I am hesitant about probing into the recent past. All questions relating to the exact circumstances of her departure from home on that Sunday morning in June are blocked with a half-smile, a gesture, a shrug; and I have been cautioned not to press her too hard. So I hold back.

For all that, there are things I should dearly like to know. How and where, for example, did she spend the Sunday night? How and why did she turn up at Vista Cottage, Hindhead, at noon on the Monday? Where did she obtain the thirty pounds in cash she had on her when found—quite apart from the amount she had already paid to Mrs Smithfield?

Her manner indicates that she doesn't remember and never will. According to the experts, such mental gulfs are common in these cases. This I accept. What I find harder to stomach is the new order of things that seems to have evolved from the episode. Aside from the fact that I no longer feel in command of my own career, my own future, there is the inescapable drawback that a vital emotional outlet has been permanently denied to me. I feel hemmed in, trapped, mortified: less than a man. Every move, however innocent, that I now make is being quietly dissected, it seems; analysed for impurities. An over-sensitive reaction, possibly. But one can't help one's inner feelings.

Behind it all, inevitably, lurks the major irritant: the unresolved matter of the photograph.

When the print finally came back from police custody, it was Peter who took charge of it. Since it belonged to him, this was only right and proper and I could raise no objection, although I felt at the time that a full discussion of its merits as a likeness would have been desirable in view of all that had taken place. I seemed, however, to be in a minority of one. Nobody else showed any inclination to chew it over further, which again is understandable: by that time the topic was threadbare and there was a kind of general unspoken agreement to let it rest.

I did contrive to snatch another look at the print before Peter carried it off to his bedroom. Regardless of what I now know about drug side-effects and my own three-year mental blindness, I feel bound to say that in an essential respect my view remained unaltered. Even allowing for a continual process of change in Sara's features, covering the period when the photograph was taken, it still appeared to me that as a pictorial record it was unconvincing . . . to put it as mildly as I know how. Since that time, no opportunity has arisen to reinforce or dispel my doubts. On several occasions I have riskily carried out a hasty search of likely hiding places in Peter's room, but the print would appear to have gone astray.

Its loss is no doubt academic. Whether or not anybody agrees with me about it is now irrelevant. Purely for my own satisfaction, I should like to study it again, that's all. But what can one do? By general tacit consent, the matter is closed, done with. Perhaps, after all, it's better that way.

POSTSCRIPT

Since I wrote the foregoing, there has been a development.

It came about two weeks ago, at the start of February. Having fallen victim to the somewhat virulent brand of 'flu that decided to drop in on us from the Far East, Carol was confined to bed for several days and Sara stayed at home to nurse her. For three days she was quite poorly, but on the fourth morning there was an improvement, and in response to demand I agreed to leave the store early to take over the hot-drinks-and-aspirin duties, enabling Sara to accompany Debbie on a crucial shopping trip to the West End. Debbie, to our surprise, had decided to switch jobs, and wanted help in choosing a special outfit for her impending interview by a panel in connection with a library cataloguing post at London University. Peter, back in France, was unavailable.

By arrangement, I got home at lunch-time and they left for town almost immediately. 'You'd better expect us when we get back,' Sara said as she offered a cheek to be pecked at. 'It's the late shopping day, so we shan't rush. You will keep an eye on Carol? She seems to be over the hump, but she'll need attention.'

'That's what I'm here for,' I said shortly. Her assumption that I needed guidance in every triviality had been irking me increasingly for some time. True to my new role, I did my best not to let resentment show, but there were times when the effort was almost too much for me and I suffered a kind of ringing in the ears that was disconcerting. This was one of the occasions. I saw them off from the porch, waving genially to them down the street, and then came inside and leaned against the lobby door, breathing strenuously to control the turbulence.

When I felt calmer I looked in on Carol, who was sleeping. I went downstairs again to tackle some of the bookwork I had brought home with me, paying repeat visits to the bedroom every half-hour or so to check on the patient. At about four-thirty she registered my appearance and asked drowsily for some hot lemon. When I brought it, she clasped the tumbler for a long time, staring at it, until I asked her whether she wanted the contents cooled a little. She shook her head.

'I was just thinking.'

'If it hurts that much, I'd be inclined to give it up.'

The look she turned on me was one that I couldn't interpret. Hostility lurked, and yet it didn't seem to be directed specifically at me. It bordered more upon self-dislike. A little perturbed, but pretending to notice nothing, I added lightly, 'Me, I ditched the habit quite a while back. Life's much simpler without it. Like a biscuit to munch, or anything?'

She shuddered under the bedsheet. 'Couldn't touch a thing.'

Returning for the glass a short time later, I found her asleep on her side with the electric blanket full on. Her face glistened with sweat. A handkerchief, soaked and crumpled, lay on the floor beside the bed. Lowering the blanket control, I went softly to the chest of drawers on the far side of the room to find some clean linen.

The right-hand side of the centre drawer was occupied by a pile of laundered handkerchiefs, female-sized and useless. The rest seemed to be taken up by folded under-wear. Thinking I might come across a headscarf that could be pressed into service, I uprooted some of the garments and they fell out of their creases, sliding into a chaotic heap at one end. With a stifled curse I lifted out the lot of them, intending to re-pack the drawer. I didn't fancy any snide comments about my domestic efficiency. I had enough of that kind of thing to put up with on other fronts.

About to start refolding a vest, I noticed that a wad of papers had been exposed at a rear corner of the drawer. I hesitated, though not for long. The thought at the back of my mind was that here might lie some explanation of Carol's apparent disquiet. After a quick glance towards the bed, I examined the top document, a sheet of pale blue notepaper half-covered with italic handwriting. Somehow I expected it to be from the Rev. Lionel Gooch: an invitation, possibly, to help out at the Parish Supper, a mundane request translated by adolescent intensity into something more heartfelt and therefore to be hoarded. But the signature, midway down the page, was not that of the curate. The letter was signed, *With love, Angela*, the name being heavily underscored in a riot of purple ink.

Angela? I had never heard mention of her. A school chum of Carol's? Cautiously removing the sheet, and keeping my body between it and the bed, I scanned the scrawled lines from the top.

. . . understand what you're aiming to do, and I must say I don't blame you. Count on me! You can arrive any time you like, no problem — I'll keep a room vacant. These days we're never full, alas. Stay as long as you want, or need to. As you know, we're very secluded and you wouldn't be bothered by anyone. Just bring nightwear and a few necessities. If cash is an obstacle for any reason, I can sub you for a week or two. I haven't forgotten . . .

Sounds of stirring came from the bed. I looked round casually. Carol was resettling herself, though not to the extent of turning. Waiting until she was motionless once more, I turned back to the letter, this time reversing the sheet and reading from the beginning.

My dear Sara, Many thanks for getting in touch — thrilled to hear from you after all this time, but naturally sad to learn of your marital hassles. Recalling my time with Reg, I can imagine how you must feel. Men! I'm rather glad I've never been introduced (or even mentioned??) to your insufferable Ralph: makes what you're asking a lot easier to agree to . . . see what I mean? Shades of St Helen's and the infamous Miss Parkhurst — no, I mustn't start reminiscing. This is just to confirm that I absolutely understand what you're aiming to do, and I must say . . .

The sheet of notepaper began to shake in my fingers, so violently that it fell back into the drawer. I could feel, almost hear, my heart hammering at three beats to the second. The ringing noise had returned to my ears. This made it difficult to gauge whether there was still silence in the room, but in a remote way I sensed that I was being watched. Overcoming paralysis, I swung sharply to find that Carol was in the same position, right cheek against pillow, breathing evenly in slumber, her knees — as was evident by the shape of the mound under the bed-clothes — drawn up nearly to her chin.

After a while — how long, I couldn't guess — I returned to the open drawer. The letter lay on top of the handkerchiefs, emitting its message like a radar pulse. For the first time, I took in the address punched faintly in gothic script into the top right-hand corner of the sheet: Vista Cottage, Devil's View, Hindhead, Surrey.

The second document in the wad comprised half a dozen folded sheets of flimsy paper secured by a clip. Releasing them, I found myself staring at a double-spaced typescript in a mixture of red and black. Here and there, passages had been struck out and amendments made in handwriting that, unlike the letter, was instantly recognizable to me. The prose style, too, was unmistakable. Before she was overtaken by reticence, Debbie had made a practice of showing me her literary efforts. From the opening line, I could practically hear her voice.

After the Disappearance, what we have to do is stoke up the mystery. Various ways suggest themselves. Weird finds in the garden, spooky phone-calls (see details below). We might even consider some sort of dig in the vegetable patch, if the cops don't think of it first. Every little helps. It can't do less than put Dad thoroughly on edge, and at best it could knock some sense into him. Failing that, it can serve as punishment, pure and simple. He's asked for it.

Most vital of all: THE PHOTO. Pete will be in France, so no bother from him — at least for the first day or so, until he gets back. In the meantime we can really make

Dad doubt his sanity. (Needless to say, these refinements are NOT to be mentioned to Mum. I'm certain she wouldn't approve.)

Luckily, I've got just the snapshot we need. It's one of . . .

Turning to the next sheet, I made an unavoidable crackling sound which seemed to reverberate through my head like rolling thunder. Checking behind me again, I saw that Carol hadn't budged.

. . . Mrs Carpenter in the Reference Library, taken nine years ago when she was about Mum's age and had her hair done in a similar style. She showed it to me the other week when we were talking about changing fashions, and I remarked how much it reminded me of Mum. Just a superficial resemblance, quite honestly, but enough for our purpose, I'd say. She said I could keep it if I liked, so I've hung on to it, just in case.

Mrs Carpenter has now emigrated to live with her daughter in Canada, which means she's nicely out of the way. We can show her photo to the police and say that it's Mum. It's close enough to her type of face to convince them we'd made a genuine mistake, if and when they find out it's not her. Meanwhile, Dad will be totally thrown, wondering if he's the one going crazy—because of course he'll know perfectly well it's the wrong snap although for a day or two at least he won't be able to prove it, even if he gets friends and neighbours to support him. We've GOT to be solid on this, the two of us.

There's plenty of other detail we can ad lib as we go along. The essential thing is to keep our nerve. And DON'T FORGET—so far as Mum's concerned, all she's doing is vanishing for a while. She mustn't know in advance about anything else.

For the mystery phone-call, I can brief Maureen to get through and mutter some cryptic message. She's good at voices and she can keep a secret.

The rough timetable of events . . .

A creaking sound reached me from the bed. Still grasping the typescript, I turned to meet Carol's wide-eyed gaze as she sat up against the headboard, hair spreadeagled. For a few seconds, neither of us spoke. It was like being part of a programmed computer, unable to deliver until the pre-appointed phase. Finally her lips moved, but I couldn't hear what she said.

'What?'

'I said, you weren't meant to go in that drawer.' Her voice was husky and very quiet, barely audible.

'I wasn't? You're quite sure of that?'

'They're my private things. You're not supposed to snoop.'

I held up the letter. '*Your* things?'

'Everything there was given to me.'

'For safe keeping? Or to be quietly disposed of? Which is it, Carol?'

Resting her head in an exhausted manner against the padded support, she closed her eyes and made no reply. I walked across to the bedside. Sensing my presence, she reopened her eyes to examine my face in a half-scared, half-defiant way; normally, the sight of her drawn features would, I remember thinking, have aroused in me some degree of paternal solicitude, but at that moment I was conscious only of a consuming anger. Bending over her, so that she shrank away, I flicked the letter loudly with my fingers.

'You wanted me to find it, didn't you? It's been preying on your conscience, so you thought the best way . . . You *hoped* I'd stumble on it.'

Feebly she shook her head. Striding back to the drawer, I held up Debbie's typescript, brandished it at her. 'This, too. It's all here—the full story. The scenario. Quite a small masterpiece, in its way, from our budding playwright. Right from the start she made all the running, didn't she, that sister of yours?'

With a low moan, Carol slid down the bed and lay staring at the ceiling.

'You were the one who had qualms,' I said, letting her hear my contempt. 'I see it now. At the time, I thought you were shattered by your mother's disappearance . . . but that wasn't it at all, was it? Oh, you were knocked out, sure enough, only not for the reason I assumed. It was the deception that had you worried. Right, Carol? Listen to me, damn you.'

She lay staring up at me in a kind of numb panic. I was putting the fear of God into her, and I was enjoying it. All the accumulated frustration of the past eight months gave me a flow of eloquence that I had thought was gone for good. 'My God,' I said bitingly, 'what a fool you must have taken me for. A sitting duck. How they must have chortled, those co-conspirators of yours. At least you had the grace to feel wretched about it. Now you want the best of both worlds. Having achieved what you set out to do, you were determined that I should know, so that you could shift the burden. How's that for a spot of psychoanalysis?'

Still she said nothing. Turning, I ransacked the drawer again. Several thicknesses of tissue paper covered the base of it, and when I lifted the corner where the documents had been, a small buff envelope came into view. Taking it out, I raised the flap.

Both photographs were inside. The one that we had given the police, plus a genuine one of Sara. Similar as the faces were in configuration and expression, seen side by side they were as distinct as two breeds of cat. The words of Inspector Sinclair flashed across my mind. *Now that I've seen her in the flesh, I think it's a lousy photo of your wife . . .*

'Presumably,' I said slowly, continuing to study them,

'Pete either knew what was going on, or was let into the secret when he came back. He'd have to have been, wouldn't he? Otherwise he'd have queried this snap of Mrs Carpenter that was published in all the papers. He had to be involved.'

Carol's silence was beginning to get to me. I felt an overmastering need to make her speak. Walking round to the other side of the bed, I confronted her again. 'Who,' I asked, 'was responsible for making the final call to Hindhead?'

She seemed about to say something, but changed her mind. It was very nearly dumb insolence. I wasn't going to fall for that, so I supplied my own answer. 'Not you, Carol. You left that to your sister, just as you left everything else. And of course, she timed it to perfection. All these months, I've been wondering what it was about your mother's reappearance that was bothering me. Now I realize. It was just too pat on cue — too hard on the heels of other events. It had to be like that, didn't it? No sense in wasting the opportunity. Between you, you'd succeeded nicely in getting an innocent woman murdered, so the time was ripe for—'

Without warning, Carol reared up. 'It served you bloody well right!' she cried, on a note of hysteria. 'You asked for all you got. I'm glad Eleanor was killed, do you hear? She was just a slag. She brought nothing but trouble.'

'What do you know about it?' All of a sudden, breathing and articulation were tricky. The ringing in my ears had worsened, drowning out what I was struggling to say.

'I know Mum was unhappy.' The words reached me faintly, from an incredible distance. 'That was good enough for me. I'm just so glad our idea worked. We reckoned on giving you a fright, but it worked out much better than that. Everything fell in our lap. The neighbours . . .'

At that point I lost touch entirely with what she was saying. I could see her there on the bed, her lips working; but for all I could hear, there might as well have been treble-glazing between us. The noise in my ears no longer seemed to emanate from bells, but from a siren whose pitch was being manipulated by ruthless operators to intolerable heights that threatened to burst my skull. It almost seemed to me, at the time, that to ease the pressure I should have done anything that suggested itself to me.

Unlike Sara, who was faking it, I now have personal experience of amnesia.

A temporary bout, it's true. Or, more accurately, a permanent one, but localized. Total enough at any rate to be bothersome. It's a weird sensation, striving vainly to recall. As with traffic accidents, there's a tendency to assume that such things don't happen to oneself: when they do, the sense of incredulous outrage borders on the ludicrous.

This I can vouch for, even though I am luckier than many. My memory has largely returned, with the exception of that insignificant portion covering the few hours between my verbal showdown with Carol and my arrival at Euston, complete with a suitcase of essentials that I had no recollection of packing. My state of shock during the period in question was undoubtedly severe. Much of the time, presumably, must have been spent on making plans, deciding what to do, where to make for.

The choice I eventually made seems to have been a reasonable one. Instinct must have governed its selection. I quite like this northern city, where I once spent a good holiday and met a girl who . . . But I mustn't even hint at its location. Because, from what I read in the papers, the police are 'anxious to trace' my whereabouts, and my own anxiety not to be traced is fully the equivalent.

More than one can play the game of keeping people guessing. Sara and the girls are no doubt worried about me. Too bad. Now they know how it feels. My ultimate reappearance, or otherwise, depends upon what I decide, freely and at leisure. Until then, they can sweat it out as I had to.

There is a good reason for not rushing things. Before making myself available to anyone at all, I'm intent upon giving myself time to dot the i's and cross the t's of this chronological account of the events of the past year: for two reasons. One is to have it all clear and straight in my mind. The other is to commit a faithful record to paper, in the not unlikely event that rival versions start to gain currency. Experience has been bitter, but it has taught me things.

Once this is done, there will be time enough to decide whether or not to resurface . . . on my own terms.

Well disposed as I am towards this city — at least I think I am, although, as with other places, its former mellow atmosphere seems to have undergone a part-conversion to rowdiness and vulgarity which intrudes increasingly on my need for peace — it costs money to stay here, and my resources are far from unlimited. The cash I evidently managed to find in the house before leaving has been sufficient to keep me in lodgings so far, but the time is fast approaching when I shall have to consider seriously my capacity to remain in hiding without additional income. If a job in London was elusive, what chance do I have here, under an assumed name?

Which is, of course, another reason for polishing off my memoir, as it might quaintly be termed. By making it readable, I may be able to sell it for publication and thus regain a measure of financial independence. It could be worth a try.

Meanwhile, what possible incentive exists for me to respond to Inspector Sinclair's bland invitation, via the Press columns, to give him a call, so that 'a few outstanding matters can be cleared up'?

His tactics are childishly obvious. Frankly, knowing him as I do, I'm surprised that he allowed himself to be persuaded to fall back upon a ruse of such transparent stupidity . . . not to say cruelty. Had I not known better, I might very well have been duped into believing that I really had harmed Carol in some way, and this I shall find it hard to forgive. GIRL'S BODY FOUND IN HOUSE. The entire national Press seems to have offered an accomodating platform for his little deception, which only goes to show how terrifyingly easy it can be to hoodwink a large number of people all at once. The similarities between their various treatments of the 'story' indicate that Sinclair must have engineered the distribution of a blanket handout. The opening paragraph of the *Clarion*'s account was typical.

> The body of a 16-year-old girl, Carol Brent, was found yesterday in bed at her home in South-west London. She had died from severe head injuries apparently caused by a heavy metal tray, bloodstained, that was found in the room. The discovery was made by the girl's mother and elder sister when they returned from a shopping trip. Police say they want to interview Carol's father, Mr Ralph Brent (40), who they believe may be able to help them in their investigations. Mr Brent, a former haulage contractor, has been missing since . . .

A crude effort. If Sara and the rest of them are so keen that I should reappear, surely they could have dreamed up something a little more convincing and a lot less nauseating. Did they really think I should fall for such drivel?

The exercise, in my view, bears the hallmark of

another of Debbie's fantasies. If and when I decide to see them all again, I shall have to speak firmly to my elder daughter about this over-active imagination she seems to have inherited from someone. It could lead her into serious trouble.

If you have enjoyed this book and would like to receive
details of other Walker mystery titles,
please write to:

Mystery Editor
Walker and Company
720 Fifth Avenue
New York, NY 10019